"Stay Silent"

A Refugee's Escape from Colombia

Text copyright © 2016 by Natalie Hyde

Published by Clockwise Press Inc., 56 Aurora Heights Dr. Aurora, ON Canada L4G 2W7

www.clockwisepress.com

christie@clockwisepress.com   solange@clockwisepress.com

10 9 8 7 6 5 4 3 2 1

Library and Archives Canada Cataloguing in Publication

Hyde, Natalie, 1963-, author

"Stay silent" : a refugee's escape from Colombia / Natalie Hyde. (Arrivals)

Includes index.

Issued in print and electronic formats.

ISBN 978-0-9939351-9-0 (paperback).--ISBN 978-1-988347-01-1 (pdf)

1. Gómez, Paola--Juvenile literature. 2. Refugees--Canada--Biography--Juvenile literature. 3. Refugees--Colombia--Biography--Juvenile literature.4. Immigrants--Canada--Biography--Juvenile literature. 5. Women human rights workers--Canada--Biography--Juvenile literature.

I. Title.

FC106.C65H94 2016   j305.48'40971   C2016-905562-0
                         C2016-905563-9

The text in this book uses OpenDyslexic and Montserrat typefaces. Cover art by Fruzina Kuhari, Yellow Bird Studios
Back cover photo courtesy of Paula Gomez
Book design by CommTech Unlimited

"Stay Silent"

A Refugee's Escape from Colombia

Natalie Hyde

CLOCKWISE
PRESS

For my father, whose ancestors made the
courageous decision to leave their homeland for
a better life in what was not yet Canada.
— N.H.

Table of Contents

Author's Note 6

Foreword 7

Prologue 10

Chapter 1 12

Chapter 2 19

Chapter 3 29

Chapter 4 36

Chapter 5 46

Chapter 6 58

Chapter 7 70

Chapter 8 79

Chapter 9 89

Chapter 10 99

Chapter 11 109

Chapter 12 118

Chapter 13 123

Photos 77

Timeline 132

Resources 134

How Kids Can Help 136

Acknowledgments 137

Index 138

Author's Note

It is difficult for anyone to leave their homeland and try to start a new life somewhere else. What would make that situation worse would be knowing that you can never go back. And what did you do to deserve losing your friends, family, home, job, and future? You stood up for a murder victim and tried to stop a horrendous act from happening again.

That is what Paola Gomez did and that was the price she paid when she couldn't possibly stay silent after a young life was snuffed out. Her story is one of strength, courage, and the never-ending search for justice.

Although much of the dialogue in the book is quoted directly from interviews with Paola, some has been recreated based on the oral history provided to improve context and narrative flow. Some details have been left out for the safety of Paola and her family.

Stay Silent...Never!

Foreword

I always had big dreams; I always looked at the world through my very particular lenses; I was different and felt like I never fit in. I always questioned why a child would need to live in a state of fear and anxiety. I wondered why being a girl was so hard. I asked myself why there was so much violence around me. I certainly never played with princess dolls or tried to be one. I was quiet, and most of the time, I was fearful or sad. Growing up, I never felt many other "nice" feelings, except for the happiness that came from hugging my grandma.

During my teen years and while reaching adulthood, I realized that it was time to speak up. I knew that my role was to be an instigator of change. I promised myself I was going to be a voice for those who did not have one, and if I could not fulfill that mission, at least I was going to make sure to have my own voice heard.

Soon I started gaining confidence. I liked not fitting into the conventional society. I was totally

OK with not being part of what it was to be "normal."

Now that I think back, I can see that I was a caterpillar, and I can recall becoming a butterfly; my wings were made of words and my heart was filled with voice...

I felt unbreakable! Soon I learned that in the context of Colombian society, being a young woman with a voice and wanting to change the world made me vulnerable. It put me in danger. However, I could not stop. That same vulnerability was the exact reason why I needed to keep going.

As painful as those chapters in my life were, I've learned from my past experiences. They've allowed me to see the world through the eyes of someone who knows pain but also one who knows hope and who has learned love and respect.

Canada has taught me about generosity. It's also taught me about the importance of being socially and civically responsible. As a member of this society, I have the obligation to check my own privileges and I have the responsibility of being an ally—an ally in amplifying the voices of those who have experienced violence and oppression.

By being declared a refugee, Canada has offered to protect my life and my family. I am forever thankful. I am aware of the privilege of protection that was given to me and that many of my brothers and sisters did not and will not have access to it.

Since the privilege that I have is based on a world full of power imbalances and government-built invisible walls, I also feel I have an obligation, a responsibility. My responsibility is to continue using my voice and my art to discuss oppression. I will continue using the mediums and platforms that I know and I will continue to challenge myself to go one step further and explore how to be a better citizen and a better human being.

I will continue to build community through art and I will always be a friendly neighbour willing to say "welcome" to newcomers.

We still need many more allies. We still need more people to believe that social justice is for all and that change is necessary. This is a process that is done one reader, one heart at a time. I hope you can join me.... in never being silent when witnessing injustice.

— Paola Gomez

Prologue

The hotel room was dingy and dark despite the rising sun. Paola watched the clock tick slowly on. In only a few minutes she could call over to the refugee reception organization, Vive La Casa, to see if today was the day she would get her immigration interview. She had been waiting for six weeks.

Paola checked the clock again. The office at Vive La Casa would now be open. She picked up the receiver and dialed.

"Hello?"

"Hello, this is Paola Gomez. I am calling to see if I have an appointment for an interview with Immigration Canada."

Paola could hear the flipping of papers on the other end.

"Okay, we just received a new list of appointments yesterday. Just a minute..."

Paola's heart was beating. *Please let it come today.*

"Yes, I see your name here. You have an appointment June 5th. This is a list of what you need to bring..."

Paola barely heard the rest of the conversation. Her thoughts piled on top of each other and her breath came in ragged gasps as she processed the news—on June 5th, 2004, she would cross over the border into her new home.

Chapter 1

Paola was supposed to be in her room concentrating on her schoolwork—the workload in grade seven was heavy—but she could hear the sound of a fight and another wail from her mother. She tried to block the sounds out, but they invaded her head even when she covered her ears with her hands.

She re-read a line of poetry from her book and it spoke to her and lifted her up. She willed it to push out the dark, heavy feeling that weighed her down—that feeling that rose up out of her anger with her mother. Why wouldn't she just leave him?

The noise subsided and Paola dared to remove her hands. Was it over?

She crept to her bedroom door and listened. All was quiet. She breathed again.

She went back to her bed and reluctantly put her poetry away and took out her schoolwork. She had to tackle the research project that was due the following week. Her teacher said they could choose any subject to research, and as she sat there, twitching at any sound in the house, terrified that the hitting was going to start up again, she knew what she was going to do.

"Have you started your project?" her friend Monica asked her as they walked home after school the next day.

Paola nodded. "I'm going to make a plan for how to design and run a shelter."

"An animal shelter?"

"No, a shelter for street kids."

Monica wrinkled her nose. "Who needs a shelter for them? My dad says those kids get what they deserve and there's too many of them on the streets of Colombia anyway. They never amount to anything. You should do your project on coffee farming. With your father's successful plantations, it should be a breeze. Why bother doing all that work on something that no one cares about?"

Paola felt as if someone had punched her in the stomach. How could anyone think that a child on the street got what they deserved? No one deserved to scavenge in garbage bins for food, and sleep, shivering, in an alley. Anyone could fall between the cracks and end up on the streets. Sometimes, the streets might be better than what was going on at home. That was something Paola often thought when she heard the hitting and crying in her own home.

Monica peeled off to go to her house and Paola continued on alone. As she neared her house she heard it—the muffled sobs of her mother. She felt those sobs right in her bones and it ached. Paola turned around immediately and headed away from the house. There was no way she could stand listening to those sounds again, so she headed to the one place where she felt safe—her grandmother's.

"I just want it to stop, Mamita," she said, her anger coming out in tears.

"You mustn't cry, Paito. Here, I have made your favourite dish," her grandmother said, passing her a plate.

Paola took a big spoonful of the rice and beans. It tasted so good that she didn't say anything while she finished. How her Mamita managed to cook such wonderful meals with so little money mystified her, but there was always something special for her when she went there.

Sometimes her grandmother would tell her stories of how it was when she was a girl. She told the stories with great drama and expression and Paola loved the emotion that she put in her tales; it made them come to life. The stories were not always happy though. Times back then were tough, but her grandmother was tougher.

Other times they would sit together and listen to Mamita's favourite soap opera on the radio. Paola loved listening to the program—the characters led such exciting lives, but no matter how complicated things got, they always found a way out of the problem. Paola wished that solutions to her family problems were found so easily.

"Why doesn't she take us away, Mamita?" Paola asked, putting her empty plate in the sink. "Why doesn't she pack up me and my brothers and go somewhere else?"

"Maybe," her grandmother said slowly, "she has nowhere to go."

"But there has to be somewhere! We could get our own place, our own apartment."

"Paito, this is a small town and everyone here knows your father and knows that he is a successful coffee farmer. He has respect and power. Why would a woman leave such a man?"

"If he is so successful, why do we live in a house full of holes where bats fly around my room every night?"

Her grandmother sighed. "Your father is very...careful with his money."

"You mean cheap."

"Paito, you should not speak about your father like that."

Paola sat in silence. She hated not being able to tell anyone what happened inside the walls of her house. It was not what it seemed on the outside. But she also knew that she was one step ahead of those kids living on the streets: hungry, cold, and in danger. She had a roof over her head, food on the table, and her Mamita when things got too bad.

"I want to do something to change the way things work," Paola said, moving her chair over beside her grandmother's.

Her grandmother worked a comb through Paola's unruly curls, patiently untangling her hair.

"That would be good, but how will you do that?"

"I'm going to become a lawyer and change the laws. I'm going to build shelters for street kids. I'm going to make a difference."

Her grandmother smiled and nodded. "Then you should. But right now you need to go home. Your father will be angry if you stay any longer."

Paola reluctantly gathered up her school

bag and said goodbye. She walked home slowly, dreading having to face her father's stony anger and her mother's red and downcast eyes.

Leave him! she wanted to yell at her mother, but nothing was ever said and nothing was ever done. In silence she went to her room, closed the door, and vowed that when she was older, she would never feel this powerless again. She would make changes. She would make sure there was always a place for frightened women and forgotten children.

Paola pulled out her project again. She mapped out how the building should look: small rooms for sleeping but with space for children to stay with their mothers, an eating area with tables and chairs, a large kitchen, and a play room.

Next she wrote out what services would be provided, including legal counsel, job training for the women, nutritious meals, and medical help.

Paola gave it more thought. People should be able to talk and visit, she thought, because there is a lot of loneliness when you carry a secret as big as her family did.

And play, she added, thinking of what she would want if her mother were strong enough to take them away to such a place. Play for the children—art classes, music, plays, and stories, because they were, after all, still children.

She worked hard on her project, making it as comprehensive as she could. When Paola got her report back a few weeks later, she didn't even notice what mark she got, she was too anxious to get it home and put it away somewhere safe. It was going to be her inspiration. The thought of building and running such a place excited her and banished the helpless feeling. She suddenly thought she could accomplish anything. Those words and pictures would be what she needed to remind herself to work hard at school so that she could be accepted into law school and start making a difference in Colombia. It would be her roadmap out of this life of secrets and misery.

But roadmaps don't always have straight lines.

Chapter 2

I *can't believe I'm here.* Paola thought as she stood in front of the three-story white building in downtown Armenia in September of 1994. The words over the door that read Universidad Le Gran Colombia made her stomach flip with excitement.

Six years of study will fly by, she told herself to calm her nerves at the mountain of work facing her. *And then you can start to change things and make a difference.*

Paola pushed through the doors with the other students and made her way up the steps to the registrar's office to pay her tuition. Her father had given her half the amount and her uncle the other half. Her plan was to take the bus each morning to the campus in Armenia from her town of Quimbaya and then go home again each night for her meals.

After her first day, Paola headed home, excited to share her experiences and tell her family how big and important the university was, but her father had news.

"This is not going to work out," he told Paola

that night. "If you are old enough to go off to university, you are old enough to take care of yourself. I've given you money, now you are on your own. You need to find a job and a new place to live."

It was a bombshell for Paola. She was only sixteen and because of her father's status in town, she had never worked at any job before. It would not have seemed respectable for the daughter of a successful farmer to have to work. Now she had no job skills, no experience, no money, and nowhere to live.

As usual, her mother said nothing. That made Paola angrier than she had ever been before. Why wouldn't her mother stand up for her?

"Mamita, may I stay with you for a while?"

Paola was back at her safe haven, her grandmother's house, while she tried to get settled for school. It was hard, though, because her grandmother did not have much money and Paola did not want to be a burden on her. It was time to find a job and a new place to stay.

Paola learned that there was a program set up by Armenia's City Hall to help students looking for a place to stay while they studied. She hoped she would qualify.

"I'd like to apply for a room in residence," Paola told program director, Bertha Maria.

"Student residences are only for our rural students who need financial help. Do you live on a farm?"

"No, not exactly. My father is a farmer, though."

"What do you mean, not exactly?"

"Well, our house is in town, but I really need somewhere to stay."

Ms. Bertha Maria leaned back in her chair. "Why can you not stay with your parents?"

Paola swallowed hard. "My father says I cannot live at home anymore...that I need to move out and get a job. I have nowhere to go."

Ms. Bertha Maria clicked her mouse and stared at her screen.

"As it happens, there is a room free. It costs 120,000 pesos per month and you do have to share with other students. Is that okay?"

Paola nodded and let out a huge sigh of relief.

It took a while to find a job but finally she was hired on full time as a financial advisor. The pay was decent, so she would be able to cover the rent, a bit of food, and her books and supplies.

The daytime hours meant she could still attend night classes.

It was with a huge sense of pride that Paola held her first pay cheque. It symbolized not only her freedom and independence, but also her strength to support herself.

After she had paid all her bills, she still had a little left over and she knew just how she was going to spend it—she wanted to treat her two little brothers still living at home to the chocolate milk powder they were seldom allowed to have, and to buy a gift for her older brother's new baby girl. Her niece was going to have the most beautiful outfit she could find.

With a job and a new place to stay, it was time to get down to business.

Paola's days were long and hard. She started at six in the morning to leave for work. She worked all day at the insurance company and then headed off to the Universidad to attend a full course load of evening classes, often working until midnight or later. Her first semester consisted of foundation courses, giving students an overview of the history of law—Roman law, Civil law, and how and why it developed. Although she was one of the youngest students, she absorbed the information quickly, rarely taking notes and being the first to leave exams. The year flew by.

"You look tired, Paito," Paola's grandmother told her. "I'm glad your first year is over—I think they worked you too hard in your studies."

"It wasn't my classes, Mamita, it was trying to work full time all day *and* having a full course load at night."

"Well then, I don't think you should go back to work when school starts up again. It's too much."

"But I need the money," Paola said. "There's tuition and books, not to mention rent and food."

"Ask your father," her grandmother said, an edge in her voice. "He should be helping you."

Paola's shoulders drooped. "I don't think he will."

"You need to ask him. He's been a bit mellower lately since the good coffee crop."

Paola didn't relish speaking to her father about money, but her grandmother was right. She was going to burn out if she continued working and going to school.

Paola gathered her things to go.

"Wish me luck," she said, giving her grandmother a hug.

"Be brave."

After dinner, Paola carefully broached the subject with her father for some financial help for the next year. To her relief, he agreed to give her what she had been paying in rent.

But there was still one small problem. Paola was no longer in the student residence and had to try to find a bachelor apartment for the same amount as the cheaper residence. It was impossible. The cheapest apartment she could find was another 50,000 pesos per month, but she took it. There was no chance that her father would give her any more money, so it was hard to focus on her studies when she had to choose between buying a textbook or buying food. She often went hungry.

Her money problems seemed to multiply. She used the money that was supposed to pay for her second-term tuition to make up the shortfall in her rent. When it came time to pay for school, she had to confess to the registrar that she was short. It was an immense relief when they offered her a credit note for the outstanding tuition. She hoped her father would help her out a bit more.

He had something else in mind.

"You know how I have always been interested in real estate," her father told her one weekend when she came home for a visit.

"Yes," she said cautiously.

"Well, I've bought an apartment in Armenia as an investment. You need to leave your bachelor apartment and move in, so it will save me the rent money I am giving you."

"But I like the bachelor. It's really close to the university and all I need," Paola said.

"This place is bigger and nicer."

Paola argued that the bachelor apartment was just fine and that this new place meant she would have to take the bus, but her father was adamant.

Knowing she didn't have the energy to work full time and go to school again, she gave in. She gave notice at her bachelor and packed up, excited to at least be moving to a better place and happy that her father seemed to want to help her succeed in her career.

Her father arrived to help her move her few things to the new place. She loaded them all on the truck, except for her ceramic frog collection. That she put in her father's car to make sure the figurines didn't break on the trip. Finally, she turned in her key to her landlord.

Then the unbelievable happened.

"Unload the truck," her father told the driver.

"What do you mean? We just loaded it," the driver asked, looking with confusion from Paola to her father.

"Unload the truck and leave her stuff here," her father said, pointing to the ground.

Stunned, the driver unloaded Paola's belongings onto the sidewalk, left them in a pile, and drove off. Her father removed her frog collection and placed it next to her other bags.

"You always want things your way. Well, that doesn't work with me," he said, then got in his car and drove off, too.

Paola watched in horror as they left and the realization washed over her that this whole "new apartment" talk was just a ploy to prove that he had power over her. She sat on the pile of all she had left in the world and cried. Cried at how unfair it was that she could be treated like this, cried at her stupidity for believing her father, and cried over the realization that she was now homeless.

This is how it happens, she thought. *This is how people end up on the streets—sometimes it's not bad decisions made by bad people. Sometimes it's circumstances out of your control and betrayal by those who were supposed to take care of you.*

Paola wracked her brain trying to think of someone who could help on short notice. Then, she remembered her uncle had a truck. She called him and was so grateful that he agreed to drive the forty-five minutes to Armenia to gather her things and take her back to her grandmother's house in Quimbaya.

Even though she was relieved to be safe with a roof over her head, Paola sank into depression and couldn't get out of bed to go to school. Even her beloved poetry books couldn't bring her out of it. She tried to understand why a father who was so respected and popular could do such a thing to his own daughter.

"Paito, you need to go back to your studies," her grandmother told her after a few days.

"I can't do this anymore, Mamita."

"Yes, you can. You told me you were going to change things, fix things. That is something important. Here, take this money for bus fare to go to school until you can get a job."

Paola looked at the bills her grandmother thrust into her hand.

"Where did you get this?" Paola asked and then she noticed her grandmother's bare finger.

"No, Mamita! You pawned your gold ring?" She burst into tears at the thought of the sacrifice her grandmother had made for her. She knew then that she couldn't just quit when her grandmother was willing to give up so much for her to continue.

"I will find a new job and make this up to you," Paola told her, reluctantly taking the money.

Her grandmother hugged her.

Paola went back to her classes and stepped up her search for another job. She knew she couldn't go back to selling insurance policies. It was the sort of job that felt too much like she was cheating people. But her age and lack of experience made it difficult to find something else.

She was getting desperate. The money her grandmother got from her ring was running low and Paola hated that the tiny bit of money her Mamita had to live on was being spent partly on her.

Each time Paola began to feel helpless again, she remembered that she had to fight and prove that she didn't need her father anymore. She vowed that never again would she let herself be hurt by him.

Just when Paola was sure that the bus money was going to run out came the visit that changed everything.

Chapter 3

"You want me to be the Family Commissioner for Quimbaya?"

It seemed incredible to Paola that such a position was being offered to her. Not only was she only eighteen years old, but the Family Commissioner held an important political position, answering to the mayor. Normally it was given to someone who belonged to the ruling political party, as well as someone older and better established.

"Are you sure you have the right person?" she asked.

The man sighed. "I know this is last minute and you are," he looked her up and down, "very young, but the last commissioner had to resign suddenly and we're desperate."

"Surely there are others who are more qualified."

"Look," said the man sitting in her grandmother's house. "We know that you come from a respectable family..."

Paola tried not to roll her eyes at this.

"...and more importantly, that you are studying law. We need someone with some legal background. Can you do the job?"

Paola thought about it. She was desperate to work and make money, but the idea of being associated with one political party or another made her uneasy. There were whispers about the things that went on with party officials, whispers of corruption and dirty deals. Did she really want to be lumped in with those people?

"I can do the job," she said, "but I don't want to be affiliated with any political party. I want to remain neutral."

The man called the mayor and Paola prayed it would be acceptable. This job could solve a lot of her problems. She would be able to continue her studies, be near her family, and start to repay her grandmother.

More importantly, Paola realized that it was also a position of power and great responsibility. As Family Commissioner, she would be the person families would come to for counselling, and she would be the person women and children could turn to for support and care.

It came to her like a crashing wave that maybe she could finally make some of the changes that would ease the difficult lives of the women and children she saw begging or living on the streets every day on her way to class in Armenia.

"The mayor says okay. You can stay neutral. Can you start Monday?"

Paola showed up for her first day of work, on a spring morning in 1998, with butterflies doing a salsa dance in her stomach. She knew that a young, smart woman would not be welcomed with open arms in an office that was full of older men who liked things to stay how they were. She adjusted her skirt and tried not to let her nerves make her wobble on her high heels. She was getting leering looks for her outfit as it was.

"Well, what do we have here?"

The city official's condescending tone made Paola stiffen. "I'm the new Family Commissioner."

"You?" He gave a laugh. "But you're just a girl, a child!"

"I'm a law student and a member of this council," she said, trying to keep her anger in check, not wanting to make things awkward on her first day.

"Well, good luck, Little Flower," he said as he walked away, chuckling to himself like this was the funniest thing he had heard all day.

Paola sat down at her desk and tried to keep from shaking. It wasn't nerves now, it was anger. Little Flower? It was a deliberate show of disrespect. She bit her tongue now, but once she was a lawyer, she was going to insist on being called "Doctor," a sign of respect that all lawyers in Colombia enjoyed.

Even though she had told herself that she wouldn't go back to working all day and studying all night, that's exactly where she was again. This time though, the job wasn't as draining. Here, instead of feeling like she was taking advantage of people, as she did in the insurance office, she knew she was helping them. The better pay also meant that she could take a decent apartment and still have enough money left over for both food *and* school books.

Paola settled into the job and really started to see the need in the area. So many issues with abuse, neglect, drugs, and prostitution were ignored or hidden from society. Paola believed that they needed to be brought out into the open and discussed before any real change could happen. Part of her job was developing awareness campaigns, but she wasn't quite sure how to make it effective. The answer came to her as she headed into her office one morning.

Right beside the city hall was a radio station. What better way could there be to not only spread the word about new programs, but also open a dialogue with the very people she was put in charge of helping? She went into the station and convinced the manager to let her have a morning slot once a week. She called it simply, "Family Commissioner at Your Home."

"Today we're going to talk about domestic violence and the law," Paola started. "If you are a victim of abuse in your home, where can you go? What are your legal rights?"

"Hello?"

"Hello, caller. Do you have a question about today's topic?"

"Well, um..."

Paola could hear the tension in the woman's voice, and it sounded a bit muffled, like she was trying to speak quietly.

"If I'm worried about the safety of myself and my children, where can I go?"

Paola swallowed hard. How she wished she could tell this frightened woman that there was a safe place for her to go to escape the abuse. But just as her mother had nowhere to go, there was nothing she could offer this woman. Such places just didn't exist in Colombia yet.

"Do you have a friend or relative who could take you in?" It hurt Paola so much to offer such weak advice.

"No," came the whisper. "I daren't tell anyone. They would take my husband's side, I'm sure and—"

There was a click. The caller had hung up.

Paola felt sick to her stomach. She had the terrible feeling that for all her good intentions and hard work, she was still failing the people who needed her. She had to do better. What the area needed wasn't just talk: it needed a shelter. She hoped the woman would call back, but she never did. Paola ended the show and went back to work.

She tried to concentrate on her paperwork, but she couldn't get the woman out of her mind, probably because it reminded her of her mother's situation. She tried to bring up the idea of a shelter for women and children with other city officials, but it was shot down each time she mentioned it.

"Stick to giving advice and counselling," her colleague Edgar told her. "That's your job."

"My job is to help families."

"So get out your paperwork and point them

in the right direction, Little Flower, and leave the big stuff to the others."

"You mean the men?"

He shrugged and walked away, but his message was clear: she was just a little girl being humoured by the men wielding the real power. He was mistaken, though. Paola had already been through so much that he didn't scare her off. His words only made her angry, and when she got angry, she became fierce.

Back in her apartment she dug out the shelter project she had completed so long ago in school. She scribbled in a few changes to the kitchen and public rooms based on the laws she now knew by heart. Somehow, somewhere, she was going to make it happen.

Chapter 4

Downtown Armenia was choked with people coming and going as Paola hurried to the registrar's office to pay the new school year's tuition fees. She bumped into a group of her friends as she was heading out the doors.

"Hey, Paola! We're going for coffee. Are you coming?" Maria asked.

"No, I can't."

"Why not? Once classes start we'll be too busy for a chat. Come on," Cesar said.

"I'm sorry, but we're having a luncheon for my grandmother's birthday and I don't want to miss it."

"You have time for one small coffee, surely," James said, folding his arms.

"Really, I don't. I'm late already."

"We'll have to do it when classes start, then, okay? Promise?" Carlos asked her, giving her a quick hug.

"Promise," Paola said, giving the four of them a wave.

Out on the street, Paola headed to the bus

stop and checked her watch. She was running late. It was already 12:30. She had to get to Jairo's Place Restaurant by 1:00 and it was in the north part of the city. It seemed like forever before the bus arrived at her bus stop.

The bus pulled away from the curb and slowly wound its way through the streets lined with palms and power lines. The lunchtime traffic was heavy with motorcycles weaving in and around the red busses. As they travelled farther north, the buildings were newer and the roads wider, with orange and yellow lilies popping out from the planted concrete barrier dividing north and southbound traffic.

When she arrived at the restaurant everyone else was already at the table.

"Paola, what took you so long?" her mother said with a frown. "We've already ordered our food."

"Sorry, Mama, but the bus was slow."

She stopped to hug her favourite uncle Oscar and her younger brother Fernando before she took her seat between her cousin Christian and her grandmother. She leaned over and hugged Mamita tight.

"Happy birthday, Mamita!"

"Thank you, Paito. How are your studies

going?" her grandmother asked.

"Good. I've just registered for this semester."

"And your job?"

"It's...all right."

Her grandmother gave her a suspicious look, but she said nothing. Paola wished she could sit and have a real chat with her grandmother about how hard she was working at school and about the troubles at her new job. Her grandmother would understand her frustration, but this was not the time or place as the restaurant was noisy and crowded.

Paola scanned the menu; she was starving. Suddenly the words blurred as the menu jiggled in her hand. Everyone had gone quiet. Paola looked up and couldn't make sense of the fact that the ceiling looked like it was moving. Why would the ceiling be moving?

"It's an earthquake!" Fernando said.

"Everybody out, before the building comes down on our heads!" Paola heard her uncle shout.

Paola panicked, knowing that her grandmother couldn't move too quickly, but Christian had already jumped up and was carrying their grandmother out. They all ran out behind her onto the street with the rest of the diners.

The shaking subsided and there was an eerie calm.

"Maybe it was just a small quake," her mother said, her voice shaking.

"Look down there!" Fernando said, pointing back toward the centre of town.

What looked like a cloud of dust was rising into the air. At least it looked like dust.

Just then a man ran over to where they were standing with the others.

"I heard it was a strong earthquake," he said loudly, moving on to spread the news. "An eight on the Richter Scale!"

Paola knew that an eight was bad, bad news. It hadn't felt that strong to them, but there was no telling where the epicentre was. That's where the worst damage would be—right in the middle.

Her mother grabbed her uncle's arm as a terrifying thought hit her, "Sebastian is still in Quimbaya. Is he all right? Can anyone call him?"

Her uncle pulled out his phone and tried to call.

"The phone lines at the house must be down," he said, not hearing a dial tone. "I think we should go," he added, with a tremble in his voice.

No one had to say what they were all thinking—that they prayed the earthquake had not been worse back in Quimbaya and that her brother was unharmed.

Paola helped her grandmother into her uncle's car and squished in beside her. Her mother and cousin climbed in her brother's car. The two vehicles pulled out of the parking lot and tried to manoeuvre around all the people clogging the streets. It was slow going.

That's when Paola saw the cows.

It took a moment to register that cows shouldn't be wandering in the streets.

"Where did the cows come from?" her grandmother asked.

"There are farms not too far from this part of town," her uncle said. "I think the pasture fences must have been knocked down."

Her uncle slammed on the brakes to avoid crashing into the car ahead of them. It seemed as if the whole city had emptied into the streets. Cars and motorcycles were packed with people trying to flee.

Paola wondered what kind of force was needed to uproot fence posts driven deep into the ground or knock down gates that were strong enough to hold back a one-ton cow. It almost felt as if they were on some science-fiction movie set.

As they crawled along, they could see now that the destruction was becoming worse the farther south into the city they drove. First they noticed the upper floors of buildings had collapsed down onto lower levels, turning falling boards and concrete into deadly weapons. Apartments that were still standing had huge cracks in the walls, and balconies and window frames lay littered on the ground.

As they continued, the damage grew frighteningly worse. Now entire streets had been reduced to piles of rubble crisscrossed with downed power lines. Dazed and confused people picked their way through the debris calling out names of missing friends and relatives. Others were sobbing and trying to pull trapped victims from under concrete, wood, and twisted metal.

"Please, please," a man begged Uncle Oscar through his open car window, "I need to get to Montenegro. My wife and daughter are there and I don't know what has happened to them!"

Montenegro was about halfway between Armenia and Quimbaya. If this man tried to walk there through debris-filled streets and panic-stricken crowds, it would take days.

"Get in," Uncle Oscar said. "We're headed in that direction."

Her uncle stopped several more times and soon there were eight people crammed into his little car, and another eight in her brother's car travelling behind them. People were sitting half on top of each other, but they had one thing in common: They were all desperate to get out of Armenia.

Progress was slow. Buildings that once stood high were nothing more than rubble strewn across the street, blocking their way. They kept having to turn around, trying to find another route.

When they neared the Universidad, Paola could see the destruction all around. The university buildings no longer stood where they were supposed to be. Paola worried about the fate of her friends whom she had waved goodbye to only a few hours ago. She wondered if they were all okay. Without radio or telephone, it was impossible to find out.

They crept along, impossibly slow. The sight of so much grief and destruction was awful to watch and Paola felt a growing fear about her little brother back home.

"Do you think Quimbaya is destroyed, too?" Paola asked her uncle, who was swerving around a downed traffic light on the road.

"We'll know when we get there," he said.

The drive from Armenia to Quimbaya, which normally took forty-five minutes, took them five long hours with the mass of cars trying to get out of the area, and with the stops they made helping the passengers in their cars get to their destinations. They arrived back at her parents' house to find Sebastian safe. It was a huge relief.

The effect of the earthquake in Quimbaya was minimal—only the oldest buildings had suffered any damage. And when the first aftershock hit the area around dinner time, those damaged buildings crumbled into rubble. It wasn't too bad, though. All the newer homes seemed to be all right.

The news filtering in from Armenia was not so good. Neighbours told them the quake had levelled both the fire and police departments, killing many officers and leaving the people with no protection. Over three hundred people were killed and thousands more were either injured or missing; the first aftershock had caused even more buildings to completely collapse.

Paola considered herself lucky that her town had escaped the worst of the quake.

"Have you heard anything more?" Paola's mother asked a neighbour the next day who had just arrived from Armenia.

"The situation is very bad there," he told her. "No police, no fire department, no phones, and mostly no power. Help was supposed to come from Bogota, but nothing..." he shook his head in anger, "...nothing has been done."

"What are people doing for food and water?" Paola asked, knowing how poor and desperate some sections of Armenia were, even before the earthquake hit.

"They are taking it."

"Taking it?"

"They are looting all the stores and warehouses. It's chaos. Last night the military arrived. I heard they arrested almost two hundred people and imposed a curfew, but the looting continues."

"Where are people sleeping?"

"Anywhere and everywhere. Mostly outside because so many buildings are still falling with the aftershocks and they are afraid to be near them. I heard estimates of 200,000 people without homes." He shook his head again, this time with sadness. "Even here in Quimbaya, the old houses are too dangerous for people to live in and the streets are filling up."

Paola could barely sit still. She knew she had to get back to work as soon as possible to help the newly homeless. Deep inside though, a tiny thought sprouted and started to take root—that this horrible tragedy might be the moment for something extraordinary to happen.

Chapter 5

"This one, that one, and that one over there," Paola said to the foreman pointing at several older homes in the more marginal area of Quimbaya.

"Do they all really need to come down?" he asked. "The buildings still look sturdy. They just have a crack or two."

"And what do you think is going to happen every time there is an aftershock? Those cracks are going to get bigger and the buildings will become more unstable."

"What about the people living in them? Are you just going to throw them out on the street?"

"Of course not," Paola said. "We've set up two temporary shelters in two schools."

"And who is going to build them a new home?"

"There is money coming from the earthquake relief fund. In the meantime we are making sure everyone has food, clothing, and medicine."

Over the next few months, the older parts of Quimbaya were slowly being torn down and rebuilt. In that time Paola also got word that her university classes, which had been suspended for three months, were to resume. They would be held in a high school gym in the north of Armenia because the university buildings were still too badly damaged.

Paola was excited to get back to her studies and finish her degree. Although the trip into Armenia showed a city that looked like it had been in a war, going back to class brought back a sense of normalcy.

She scanned the area outside the high school, looking for Maria, Cesar, and the others. She owed them a coffee date, and if the earthquake taught her anything, it was to not put things off.

"Have you seen Maria Aldana?" she asked a classmate.

The girl didn't answer for a moment, and then took a deep breath and said, "Didn't you hear?"

Paola felt a cold chill run down her spine. "Hear what?"

"She didn't make it. She was on campus when the earthquake hit," her classmate said, her eyes welling up with tears. "There was so much damage...she didn't stand a chance."

"What about the others?" Paola asked, whispering now, afraid to hear the words spoken aloud as if that would make them true.

"What others?"

"Cesar Mondragon. James Osorio. Carlos Naranjo."

Her classmate shook her head wordlessly, the tears streaming down her cheeks now.

Paola walked away in a daze. It couldn't be. Her friends couldn't be gone. She had promised them she would see them again. How could they all be dead?

It was a struggle for Paola to concentrate on her classes; all she could see in her mind were her friends' faces, smiling, asking her to go for coffee. Then the truth of that day hit her. If she had gone with them, she would have been caught in the concrete falling from the sky and sizzling power lines lacing the ground like venomous snakes, too.

Her grandmother's birthday lunch had saved her life.

She tried to write a poem commemorating her friends, celebrating their friendship and their lives, but her emotions were still too raw. The page stayed blank.

As she grieved for her friends and all the

others she learned had died that day, Paola felt that her life had been spared for a reason. She could not and would not waste this gift. She was going to stop just talking and dreaming about her plans and finally take action and make a real difference in the lives of the people she was hired to protect—she was going to start by opening a shelter in Quimbaya for street kids.

Paola spoke with the mayor the next day. She explained that with so many more kids on the streets because of the earthquake, this was the perfect time to open a shelter. To her astonishment, he agreed.

In June of 1999, Paola opened the New Dawn Child Protection Centre in Quimbaya. The earthquake that had ruined so many lives would now be the reason so many others would be saved. Because buildings were being rebuilt and renovated all over town, Paola was able to secure a location for the shelter and have it rebuilt to her specification.

The second floor of City Hall was now the shelter for kids. It had eight rooms, including four dormitories (two rooms for the girls and two for the boys), a room for programs and a room for one-on-one services. It could sleep twenty-four kids and accommodate up to fifty for the programs. A team of thirteen, including a secretary, a psychologist, a speech therapist, educators, maintenance personnel, and kitchen staff, kept the place running smoothly.

And of course, Paola was there almost every day. Sometimes she even slept there. The shelter was her baby and the kids there were "her" kids. She didn't care where they came from or what their parents did—she just wanted to keep them safe. She knew all too well what happened to kids on the street.

In fact, everyone knew what happened to street kids and the homeless. Every now and then, vehicles would sweep through town at night to "cleanse" it, taking every man, woman, and child found there. Drug addicts, the mentally ill, vagrants, street kids, and those in the sex trade were all targets. Once they were taken, they were never seen again.

The optimistic people in town believed those who were taken were simply arrested or dropped off outside another city's limits to become "their" problem. Others feared something much more sinister. There were whispers that "disappeared" really meant "murdered." No one said it out loud. No one wanted to be the next victim for daring to point fingers.

Paola knew that her shelter protected those kids who had nowhere else to go—protected them from drug dealers, pimps, and the "cleansings." Her team supported her when she made sure the shelter was open and fully staffed on Fridays, Saturdays, and Sundays. These were the days that women in the sex trade were busiest, as farmers came in from the countryside for the weekend. Their children were left unattended and unprotected while they worked. This was the most common time for the disappearances, so Paola made sure these kids had somewhere safe to stay, eat, and sleep.

"You've stepped in it now, Little Flower," a voice said behind her at the office.

"What are you talking about?" she asked, spinning around to face her colleague, Edgar, who was leaning in a little too close for comfort.

"The talk is that you are in a *lot* of trouble."

"For what?"

"Word is your little shelter is a violation of the town's moral code. They're going to shut you down."

"A violation in what way? It's a shelter." Paola could feel the anger boiling and rising in her gut.

"You are taking in the children of *prostitutes*."

He hissed the last word, like it was poison on his tongue.

"They are *children.* I don't care what their mothers do. They need my help and I'm going to help them." Paola practically spat the last few words, causing Edgar to step back.

"Watch your step, Little Flower. You're playing with the big boys now."

He walked away and left Paola shaking with rage. She tried to get back to work, but her mind was racing. She knew that her position gave her the power to legally create and run the shelter, but she felt vaguely uneasy and vulnerable at Edgar's implied threat.

She broached the topic during her next radio show. She asked the people of Quimbaya how they felt about the shelter.

"I think it's good that you get kids off the streets," one caller said. "Terrible things happen when they are left to themselves out there."

Paola thanked her for her call.

"It's not right," a male caller said. "What those women are doing is a sin. And their children are sinful, too. You should not encourage it."

"I don't approve of the mothers, but it's not the children's fault," a woman caller argued. "You should be commended for the work you do."

"I think it's a disgrace!" another caller said. "You are making it easy for women to be prostitutes! You are inviting them to do so!"

Paola tried to explain to the caller that no woman with other options would prostitute herself simply because there was somewhere for her kids to go. The caller was having none of it, though.

Paola sighed. Some people would not be convinced, but Paola did not let it deter her.

Back at the shelter, the psychologist, Ana Maria, cornered Paola as she arrived.

"I have an idea," Ana Maria said.

"About what?"

"About Juan."

Paola looked across the program room to where Juan and his sister Pastora were drawing with the other kids.

"I feel so bad for him," Paola said. "I'm pretty sure he is abused at home and I know he goes to school hungry most of the time. But he is so smart, caring, and mature for his age. And so talented! Have you ever heard him sing? He has an amazing voice."

"I know," Ana Maria said. "That's why I want to help him. Do you think it's possible to enroll him in music and dance class? I think it would have a big effect on his self-esteem."

Paola knew that he was the type of kid who would do a lot with a little, and she wanted to show him that if he worked hard, things would eventually get better.

"I'm sure we can find the funds somewhere," Paola said. "And if not, I'll pay for it myself. Thanks, Ana."

Paola told Juan the plan and his face lit up like a neon sign.

After that, he came to the shelter every day for a meal and then went straight to his lessons. She watched him interact with the other kids at the shelter more, his confidence soaring with each passing week. It was gratifying for Paola to see him blossom.

"We're having a recital," Juan told her a few weeks later.

"Wonderful!" Paola said. "I'll make sure I'm there!"

Juan beamed. Then his face sobered a little. "Do you think my parents will come?"

Good question, thought Paola. *Would they?*

"You'll have to ask them," she told him, hoping against hope that they would.

The day of the performance, Paola scanned the audience and was amazed to see his parents there. His mother sat, eyes downcast next to his unsmiling father.

The recital began with drums and guitar solos. Then it was Juan's turn to sing. His voice rose and swelled and filled the room. It was hard not to be touched by the emotion he put into the song. Paola looked over and saw his mother reduced to tears. His father's mouth hung open in surprise.

When he finished, Juan ran to his mother, hugged her, and cried with her. Paola knew that moments like these were why she did what she did every day.

When she got back to the shelter after the performance, Edgar was waiting for her. And he didn't look pleased.

It brought her back down to the ground with a bump after the happiness and excitement of the recital.

"I am getting complaints," he said, after a quick nod of his head, meant to be a greeting.

"About what?" Paola asked, knowing full well what it was all about.

"About the kids you have here. They are..." He lowered his voice. "...delinquents. This is not the sort of people we are here to help. Their mothers are sinful women."

"I am here to help *all* the people of Quimbaya. Including the children of prostitutes," she said forcefully. "Children have no choice or control over what their parents say, believe, or do." She trembled with emotion, remembering how helpless and ashamed she had been of her own parents' behaviour.

Just then, Juan came up to her.

"Excuse me, Ms. Gomez," he said.

"Oh, Juan, congratulations on your performance. I was so impressed."

Juan smiled shyly beside her as Paola introduced him to Edgar.

"I just wanted to say thank you," Juan told her. "I am so happy that my mother knows how it feels to be proud of me."

Paola hugged him. "I'm proud of you, too."

After Juan left, Edgar said, "You are too soft on these kids. That has to change."

"Too soft? These kids have rarely heard a kind word their whole lives...not from their families, not from their neighbours, and certainly not from city officials." Paola's eyes blazed.

"They need discipline, not hugs and kisses. I have ordered that room over there..." He pointed to a storage space. "...be turned into a reflection room."

"Reflection room?"

"Yes. When they act up, they will go in there to...reflect. Workmen will start tomorrow."

Paola said nothing. She also said nothing when the workmen finished building what amounted to a cell for children. And she also said nothing to her staff or the children because she had no intention of ever putting a child in it.

Not even a child like Wilfred.

Chapter 6

Kids like Wilfred were the very reason Paola worked so hard to provide a safe place for street kids. She first met him on the streets, at night, during one of the shelter's Operation Friendship missions. *Operacion Amistad*, as they called it in Spanish, was a chance to talk to the street kids face to face and offer them some hot chocolate and buns. She told them of the activities and the warm, safe place to sleep the shelter offered, and encouraged them to come.

Wilfred had come. At twelve years old, he carried the evidence of his difficult life in the large scar that crossed his face. It wasn't a surprise to anyone that he struggled with anger issues. But Paola never even considered putting him in the jail-like "reflection room." She encouraged him to join in the activities and hoped that kindness, understanding, and time would help him.

But time was something that Paola couldn't guarantee she would have. There was a new budget on the horizon. Paola feared that with all the controversy about the children she was helping, funding for the shelter would disappear. She worried that Wilfred and the others would be back on the streets.

Only a few months before the elections and just when she was really getting concerned, an unexpected solution dropped into her lap.

The mayor dropped by her office with a surprising request.

"Paola, how do you feel about becoming deputy mayor?" he asked her.

"Deputy mayor?" Paola asked, astonished. She had no doubts that she could do the job, but at only twenty-one years old, it would be hard to get any respect from the older people who would have to report to her.

"Just temporarily while I'm away. Do you think you can handle it?"

"Of course I can!" she answered, her passion and self-confidence bubbling to the surface.

He laughed. "Well don't get into trouble. Keep a low profile and everything should just run smoothly on its own."

Paola nodded.

But deep down, she had no intention of keeping a low profile. There were too many important things she could accomplish once she was in power. First on her agenda was funding. City elections and the new budget were only a few months away so there was no time to waste. As her first task as deputy mayor, Paola redirected money to keep the shelter running and extended all the contracts of the shelter staff.

The office was quiet and she was so focused on filling out all the proper paperwork that she didn't even hear Edgar come in.

"Where are the keys to the truck?" he asked.

"Here," she said, pulling the keys out of a drawer in the mayor's desk. "Who needs the truck?"

"Never you mind, Little Flower. Just give them to me."

Paola tried not to show Edgar how angry that nickname made her, especially now that she had graduated and was officially a lawyer. Paola's hand closed around the keys as she asked again, "Who needs the truck?"

"It's official business," he said, a snarl starting to curl on his lips. "And if you know what's good for you, you'll stop asking questions and hand them over."

Paola didn't like the look in his eyes. She decided it was not worth jeopardizing all the important things she was doing as deputy mayor by getting into a fight over a truck.

She handed Edgar the keys. After he left the office, she hurried to the window to see whom he had given them to. She squinted at the truck to see who was driving it away.

She recognized the uniforms, and then caught a glimpse of their faces. She suddenly understood what was going on. They were going to do a "cleansing."

Paola froze in horror by the window. She she had just helped to hand the keys to those murderers. As Paola stood there, with her mind reeling, Edgar stormed back into the office.

"And what is this?" He waved an angry fist with a memo in it. She left the window and moved back to her desk.

"What is what?" she asked calmly.

"A notice that my project funding fell through. What happened to the money I had set aside for this?"

Paola took the notice and read it. "Oh," she said, "that's because you mistakenly took money from the earthquake relief fund for your own purposes. That money is supposed to go toward rebuilding the parts of town that were affected by the earthquake, not for your personal pet project. People are homeless and depending on this money to get back in a home."

Edgar's face reddened. Paola folded her arms.

"You are making a big mistake," he said quietly and left the room.

Paola rubbed her temples. Although she acted tough, deep down it was unsettling to hear the stories of violence and corruption that ran through all levels of government. She needed to get out of there. She headed back to the one place that made her feel good—the New Dawn shelter.

Walking through the doors of the shelter, she could see there was trouble. Wilfred was in a rage and throwing art supplies against the wall. Paola ran over to him.

"Wilfred, calm down."

She did her best to keep her voice low and soothing. Yelling now would only escalate the tension.

"Talk to me, buddy. What happened?"

Wilfred paused in his rampage and looked at her. His eyes started to well up with tears, and then, as if a veil had been pulled down over his face, the look disappeared and was replaced with a blank stare. He got up and ran from the room, into the hallway, and out of the building.

Paola turned to Ana Maria. "What set him off?"

"Hard to say. He was fine all morning and then someone said something about his picture..."

Paola nodded, knowing that's all it would have taken—a careless comment about his drawings, his clothes, his looks. He never lasted more than a few days at the shelter before he took off again.

Paola wasn't really sure where he went, but he usually returned again after a few days. When Wilfred struggled, it took almost nothing to light his fuse. Other days, he was easygoing and friendly and actually quite funny. Paola loved seeing this side of him come out. She hoped that with more time, the fun side would come out more often than the angry side.

Paola turned to the other kids in the shelter who sat quietly after Wilfred's outburst and said, "I think today, we need to...go on a picnic!"

That news was met with a big cheer. Everyone helped pack up what they would need while the kitchen staff prepared a picnic lunch.

"This is a great idea," Ana Maria said as they headed to the park. "Not many people would do stuff like this for these kids."

"They deserve a normal childhood, too," Paola said simply.

It was a beautiful afternoon and a welcome break for everyone. But when Paola returned to the shelter, a surprising package awaited her.

"Why is this baby back?" Paola asked Sandra, the therapist, who was holding a six-month-old infant. "We sent him to Armenia to be placed in foster care."

"They said they can't place him."

"Why not?" Paola asked, tickling his chin and making him smile.

"Because he's sick and they can't place a child who needs so much care. He has seizures and needs medicine."

"What are we supposed to do with him?" Paola asked, her voice rising in anger. "Put him back on the streets to die?"

Sandra shrugged helplessly.

"Give him to me. If he needs care, I'll give it to him," Paola said.

"But, Paola, the medication is expensive and he'll need it for a long time."

"So what? I have money. I'm going to pay for the treatment until he is well. If I'm not going to help these children, then I might as well quit my job."

Back in her office, Paola looked at the sleeping child in the basket beside her desk. Her bravado and belief that she could do anything slipped a little as she tried to work out how she was supposed to care for a sick baby, finish the last two semesters of her law degree, and still do a job that took up hours and hours of her time.

In the end, Paola's secretary, Eugenia, agreed to take him to her house. They would take turns looking after him there. Paola cut down her hours to half-days so she could drive him to his treatments in the afternoon.

It was a grueling schedule for both of them. About a month into the arrangement, Eugenia told Paola that she couldn't do it anymore. The baby was having convulsions at night and no one was sleeping.

Paola, who was also burned out, agreed that a change was needed.

"But we are a month in, and I am not going to jeopardize what we've accomplished with his treatment so far," she told Eugenia.

Paola then turned to the only person she could think of who could help with such a young, sick child. Her mother.

But how was she going to convince her to take on such an enormous responsibility?

Paola went to the house with the baby in her arms and stepped into the kitchen where her mother was preparing lunch. And that's when the words spilled out of her mouth.

"Mom, I'm taking care of this child. But he's sick." Paola wasn't sure how her mother would react. They didn't always have the best relationship and she didn't know if her mother would help her now.

"Oh, the poor little thing," her mother said, taking the baby and cuddling him. She bathed him and dressed him and then offered him some orange slices. The little boy loved it and made little gurgling noises as he sucked the sweet juice.

Her mother was smitten. It was impossible not to love the little boy Paola called Santiago. Her mother agreed to care for the child while Paola went back to work full time. Paola was relieved. She had to admit it, she was smitten, too.

It felt good to be back at work though because there was so much to do. Sometimes Paola didn't even go home for days at a time and just slept at the shelter.

She had plans to improve and expand the art programs for the shelter kids. Her idea was to bring in artists from the community to share their creative processes with the kids and help them explore their talents. She thought it would be fun if they could work on a big mural together.

But a small piece of paper stopped her in her tracks.

"Where did this come from?" she asked Ana Maria, holding the flyer in her hand.

"It was slipped under the door. It was there when I got here this morning."

Paola held it with trembling hands. It was a notice. No, it was a warning. Someone had heard that there was to be a "cleansing" that night. Nothing made Paola's skin crawl more than that little word. It wasn't the first warning she had received, and it probably wouldn't be the last. Every few months, rumours would start and people would hide.

"Ana Maria, tell the kids they need to stay here tonight. Tell them whatever they do, they shouldn't be on the streets once it gets dark."

"Why? What's going on?"

"This is a warning that there will be a 'cleansing' tonight."

Ana Maria paled and then hurried to calmly

but firmly convince the kids to all stay for the night.

"Has anyone seen Wilfred?" Paola asked Ana Maria when she came back from talking to the kids. He had had another one of his angry outbursts that morning and had taken off for the streets again.

Ana Maria shook her head.

Paola went to Juan and a few of the older boys.

"I need you guys to do me a favour. I need you to find Wilfred and tell him he needs to stay at the shelter tonight. Tell him I don't care if he leaves again tomorrow, but he needs to stay here tonight. In fact, tell everyone you know who is living on the street to come here. We'll make room for everyone. And make sure you are all back here by suppertime."

It was early afternoon when the boys left and Paola waited anxiously for them to return. As good as their word, they came back for supper along with a bunch of other kids, some of whom Paola knew, and others she didn't. But Wilfred wasn't among them.

"Did you find Wilfred?" she asked Juan.

He shook his head. "We looked everywhere and asked everyone. Don't worry, I'm sure he'll be

all right," he told her. "Wilfred will know where
to hide."

Paola hugged Juan and let him go to supper.
She hoped Wilfred would hear the news about the
"cleansing" somehow and would show up on his
own before dark.

But Wilfred never came.

Chapter 7

Morning came and many of the kids who had come for the night stayed for breakfast before taking off again. Paola urged them to come back for some of the art programs but she wasn't sure how many would. She kept herself busy but her mind still went back to Wilfred. She hadn't heard anything more about the "cleansing" the night before. Maybe it didn't happen? She wondered if he would show up for a meal or two.

Paola slipped out of the shelter and drove to her parents' to take Santiago to a doctor's appointment and then visited with him for a while back at the house afterward. She loved cuddling him on her lap while she read some of her favourite poems to him. She couldn't believe how big he was getting and it was a huge relief to know that the medication was helping. Her mom said the seizures were less and less frequent.

"What is *he* still doing here?" Her father asked, gesturing to Santiago. He had just come in from the coffee fields and was hot and tired. "He's better, isn't he?"

Paola held Santiago close. "He's staying with us. I never said he was just here to get better. I'm keeping him. He's my son now."

Her father gave a dismissive wave of his hand and stomped off.

"Paola, you can't keep him," her mother said.

"Yes, I can," Paola said, her stubbornness rearing its head. "I'm going to adopt him and he can come and live with me at my apartment."

"You can't."

"And why not?"

"You're too young. You can't legally adopt a child in Colombia unless you are at least 25 years old. You're only 21."

Paola went silent. She hadn't thought of that.

She hugged Santiago tight. "But I can't bear the thought of losing him."

"I think I have a solution," her mother said. "I can adopt him."

Paola was stunned at the offer. But the idea that Santi would be out of the adoption system and taken care of each day was a huge burden lifted from her heart. She nodded, smiling.

Feeling overwhelmed with happiness and relief at Santiago's situation being resolved, Paola wasn't prepared for the news that waited for her back at the shelter.

Ana Maria met her at the door, her eyes red-rimmed and moist.

"What is it?" Paola asked.

"It's Wilfred."

"What about him? Where is he?"

"They found him in the park."

"What do you mean, 'found him'?" Paola asked, not wanting to hear the truth.

"Found his body."

"No!" Paola said, shaking her head. "No, no, no, no, no."

Ana Maria hugged her and they cried together.

Later that day, Paola's grief turned to anger. *Who had done this to him?* She grabbed her sweater and went out onto the streets and headed to the park.

The park seemed strangely quiet and peaceful, not like a child's life had just ended there.

"It is so sad about the boy," a voice said. A woman had walked up to Paola.

Paola nodded.

"How do these people live with themselves, doing this to others?"

"What people?"

"You know," the woman said, looking around nervously and lowering her voice. "The people who do the cleansings."

"The cleansings? You're sure that's what happened to the boy found here in the park?"

"How else do you think this happened? Everyone knew they were coming last night. Word around town is that eight others have disappeared. Who knows if their bodies will ever be found."

The woman shook her head and walked away.

Paola hadn't forgotten about the anonymous note warning of a "cleansing" the night before, but she had tried to convince herself that Wilfred's death was something else—like an accident or a mysterious illness. The idea that his life was deemed worthless by nameless men roaming the streets was too much to bear. Her anger grew.

Wilfred's funeral was an incredibly difficult ceremony to experience. He was too young to lose his life. The team from the shelter all went to pay their respects. There was something unbearably sad about a casket that wasn't full size carrying the remains of a life too short and hard.

Wilfred's mother was there, but where Paola expected to see keening and moaning, there was only a woman with a lowered head and drooping shoulders. It seemed to Paola that these horrible events had happened so often over so many years, that people couldn't even react to them anymore. It was almost expected. Paola hated the fact that she lived in a place where the disappearance and murder of street kids was normal.

Even after the funeral, Paola couldn't let go of her anger. Something had to be done. Someone had to speak the truth. Did she have the courage to be that person?

Back at the shelter Paola buried herself in her work. Keeping busy kept her mind from going to the dark place of Wilfred's death. But reminders of the twelve-year-old were everywhere: in his artwork that was still drying on screens, in the bed where he sometimes slept, and even in the dents on the wall from when he had a meltdown and threw things.

The next day, she was at the radio station for her weekly program. As she sat down to the mike and put on the headphones, she knew there was only one topic she could cover: Wilfred.

She began by just talking about the Wilfred

she knew, the tough street kid who struggled to survive, belong, and get along. Then she described her shock and horror at the news of his death.

"Hello, this is the Family Commissioner at Your Home. You are on the air," Paola said to her first caller.

"I'm sorry to hear about the young boy, but you know, we were all warned what would happen."

Paola tried to control her anger.

"So, is it okay with you that we have these 'cleansings'?" she asked the caller.

"Well, we can't stop them."

"We can't stop them if we keep ignoring them and pretending they're not going on. We have to speak up and say it's not okay with us. Don't you agree?"

"I don't know."

The caller hung up.

The phone line lit up again.

"You're on the air."

"I think you should keep your nose out of this business," a man's voice said. "You're playing with fire."

"Is that a threat?" Paola asked, but the caller had hung up.

"This is exactly why we have such a vile and

despicable practice happening over and over!" she said into the mike. "Because people feel threatened and are too afraid to say what they know. Well, I'm tired of it. I want this to stop. I don't want even one more innocent child like Wilfred to die. So I am speaking up. I know who is responsible."

And then Paola did the unthinkable. On the air, to everyone listening, she described the uniforms she had seen in the truck that day. She accused the organizations responsible for cold-blooded murder.

She named names.

The next day, the death threats started.

(left) Paola Gomez, age 16

(below right) Paola and Matthew arrive in Canada on June 5, 2004.

(below left) Paola working at the City Community Response Unit

All photos on this page courtesy of Paola Gomez

(above right) Paola facilitates a workshop for women.

(right) Paola learns English in Toronto.

(above) Paola helps children express themselves through art as part of her Sick Muse program,

(right & below) **Participating in activities with the children at the Sick Muse program.**

Photos on this page courtesy of Alex Usquiano

Chapter 8

Opening the mail became an ordeal. She wasn't sure what she'd find there.

Going home became an ordeal. She would jump every time the phone rang.

Going to work was an ordeal, as she was constantly looking in the rearview mirror.

There were whispers among the staff at the office. *Are they talking about me?* Paola wondered.

Paola looked at the pile of mail on her desk and took a deep breath. *Maybe this would be a good day*, she thought.

She began opening envelopes and pulled out forms, memos, and official letters. No hate mail. She started to breathe again.

She was down to the last piece of mail. She ripped open the plain white envelope. Inside was a piece of paper with a dark purple border. Paola recognized the design—the deep purple border on the card showed that it was a death notice, the kind given out at funerals as a memento of the deceased person with their name, date of birth and death, and maybe a few words about their life.

Only this one had *her* name on it. As if she was already dead.

Paola dropped it as if it were on fire. Her hands trembled. Her mouth went dry. She rifled through the envelopes to find the one it came in. It was printed on a computer with a smudged postmark so there was no clue as to who sent it or even where it was mailed.

She grabbed her purse and drove to her parents' house. She needed to get out of the office, calm down, and get herself back under control. And nothing made her feel more grounded than seeing her little boy, Santiago.

"Why aren't you at work?" her mother asked her.

Paola cuddled Santi on her lap. "It was a slow day so I thought I would come over."

"For what?"

Paola tried to think fast. She didn't want to worry her mother.

"Well, it's almost Santi's birthday. We need to plan his birthday party!"

"Yes, he deserves a nice party," her mother said, getting up to answer the phone. "He is doing so much better. His convulsions have all but stopped, and look how chubby he's getting!"

Santiago smiled up at Paola and her heart melted.

She was so engrossed in playing with him that she didn't even hear the phone ring a few minutes later.

"Paola, it's for you."

Paola handed Santiago over to her mother and went to the phone, wondering who would be calling her at her parents' house.

"Hello?"

There was silence on the line.

"Hello?"

"You've made a big mistake," a raspy voice said quietly. "You're going to pay for it."

"Who is this?"

"Have a nice afternoon with your parents and your little boy," the voice said before the line went dead.

Paola stood, frozen in fear, still holding on to the receiver.

"Who was it?" her mother asked.

"Nobody," Paola said.

"You're pale, Paola. Are you all right?"

"I'm fine."

Paola walked over to her mother, took Santiago in her arms, and held him tight. Her mind was whirling. The caller knew where her parents lived. Where her son lived. What if they came for her and harmed her family?

"I think I need to get away for a while," Paola said.

"Get away? What do you mean?"

"I think it would be better if I left town."

Her mother stood up and put her hands on her hips. "What is going on, Paola?"

Paola took a deep breath. "I am getting death threats. Because of the radio show."

"Because you went too far. That's what you did. You had to go and name names, and now look." Her mother paced the floor.

"It'll blow over," Paola said. "I just need to give it some time."

She wasn't sure how much time, but she knew she needed to leave. With her mother's help, she contacted a relative in a town eight hours away.

It wasn't hard getting a leave of absence from work; Paola figured they were uncomfortable with the attention the office had been getting since the day of the radio program. But it was hard leaving Santiago. She spoke to him as often as she could on the phone.

Time passed slowly. Week after week Paola kept to herself and stayed out of public as much as possible. After two months she got word that her leave was up and she needed to come back or lose her job.

She let the job go. She had to make sure no one was asking her whereabouts anymore before she could return.

Three months later, all seemed quiet. Paola's mother told her the phone calls had stopped and there was no suspicious mail anymore.

In October, Paola finally felt it was safe enough to drive home. She didn't tell anyone in town she was coming back. She was too nervous and wanted to fly under the radar for a while. The first thing she did when she got to her parents' house was hug Santiago good and tight.

"He's grown so big in three months!" she told her mother.

"Yes, and he is walking now and getting into everything!" her mother said with a chuckle. Then the smile left her face. "Are you sure you should have come back here?"

Paola nodded with more confidence than she felt. "I think the worst is over. And besides," she said, bouncing Santiago on her lap, "I couldn't stay away forever. At some point I need to face this."

She smiled reassuringly at her mother, but inside her stomach churned a little. People had long memories and she had stirred up some powerful anger. She decided to stay the night at her parents' and go back to her own apartment the next day. She thought she might feel braver in daylight.

The next few nights, Paola made sure all her doors and windows were locked tight. During the day she stayed inside with the curtains drawn. After a few days, she knew she would have to summon the courage to go out because she was out of food.

The trip to the grocery store was uneventful. A few people stopped to chat and no one really questioned why she had left or why she had returned. Either they hadn't noticed, or they already knew the answer.

She started to feel more like herself, but it was strange not to go to work and not to go to the shelter. It had been almost a month since she had come back but she still didn't think she should make contact with her team or the kids. She hoped in time maybe she could get her job back, or even just volunteer at the shelter. Right now she didn't want to risk going there and putting the kids in danger.

Instead she decided to head to Pereira, a city about a two-hour drive away, to visit friends.

She stopped at her mother's house to let

her know her plans and to see Santiago.

"You be good now," Paola told Santi with a kiss. "I'll be back tomorrow."

She headed north on highway 29Q. After going through the town of Alcala, the road wound its way up and down hills through wooded areas dotted with farms.

It was dusk. The palm trees overhanging the road made it seem even darker. As she came to a lonely stretch of road where the banks on either side of the road rose up, she saw a roadblock ahead. She stopped and her heart began to thud in her chest. The men were all wearing military clothing and had their faces covered with ski masks. They held assault rifles in their hands.

One came over to her and made a motion for her to roll down her window.

"Papers," he said.

With trembling hands Paola handed over her identification and driver's licence.

"You're the Family Commissioner of Quimbaya, I see?"

Paola realized that her papers still showed her as employed by the city, so she didn't dare contradict him by saying she no longer worked for them.

She nodded.

"Where are you headed?"

"Pereira."

"Get out of the car."

It was completely dark out when Paola regained consciousness and realized that she was alone. Alone but badly beaten.

She tried to push away the memory of what had just happened to her. She tried to forget the threats the men spewed out, that they knew who she was and what she had done. That the next time, they would kill her.

But like bile rising from her gut, the reality kept bubbling to the surface. Tears streaked down her cheeks. When she brushed them away she saw that her trembling hands were bloody. Her clothes were shredded. A quick look in the car mirror showed her face starting to swell into an unrecognizable mass with black and blue patches. One eye was almost swollen shut.

"Think, think," she whispered to herself. "Where can you go?"

Even in her shattered state she knew she couldn't go back home. The men in the ski masks knew where home was. And she didn't want to go to Pereira because they knew that's where she was headed. She couldn't risk running into them again. Ever. She knew that they had meant it when they said she wouldn't live through another meeting with them. So instead, she headed to her aunt's house another hour away.

When she knocked on her aunt's door, the swelling on her face must have worsened because her aunt didn't recognize her at first.

Paola barely slept that night. Although she could keep the memories at bay while she was awake by focusing on what she was going to do, at night her mind slipped back to the black places. She would wake up in a cold sweat and realize that the screaming she heard was from her own mouth.

The next day she called her mother.

"Where are you, Paola? You said you'd be back today."

Paola's voice quivered as she tried to get the words out, "I'm not coming home. I have to leave. I have to leave the country."

There was silence on the line.

"What happened?" her mother asked in almost a whisper.

"I was attacked last night. I thought they were going to kill me..." Paola broke off into sobs.

"Oh my goodness, Paola! Are you all right?"

"I...I will be. But not here. I can't stay."

"What are you going to do? Where will you go?"

"I need you to send me some money. Tell Dad I will sell my car to him, half price. I just need cash for a plane ticket. Oh, and can you send me my passport?"

"Plane ticket? Passport? How far are you going?"

"I have to leave the country. Tomorrow."

"But, what about Santiago?"

Paola could barely get the words out: "Tell Santi I love him. And I'm sorry."

Chapter 9

"Hi, Aleida?"

Although Aleida and Paola's older brother had separated and she now lived in Switzerland, Paola still felt close to her sister-in-law.

"Paola? Is that you?"

"Yes. Aleida, I'm in a bit of trouble. I need to leave the country right away."

"Oh no, what's wrong?"

"I don't have time to go into it now; I'll tell you later. But I need a favour. Do you think your friend Thomas would take me in for a while?"

"Thomas Moore, in New York? You're leaving Colombia?"

"Yes, I have to leave right away."

"I'll give him a call. He's a good guy. I'm sure he'll help you. But Paola, call me when you get there and let me know that you're okay."

"I will. And thank you."

As good as her word, Aleida called her friend in New York and he agreed to let Paola stay with him. He asked for a sign so he would know her at the airport. All Paola had was a little toy frog that she had hanging from her car's rearview mirror. It would have to do.

The next day, Paola's passport arrived and she drove to Matecana Airport in Pereira and boarded the plane. The flight passed in a blur. The whole thing seemed unreal to her, like it was happening to someone else.

It was dark out when the plane landed in New York and Paola still had to go through customs. Her heart pounded in her chest. What if they deported her? With one wrong answer they could deny her entry and then put her back on a flight to Colombia to her certain death.

"Passport," the custom agent said, holding out his hand.

Paola handed it over.

"Why are you coming to the United States?"

"To visit a friend."

"What's this friend's name?"

"Thomas Moore."

"And where does he live?"

"New York City."

The agent looked up at her, his eyes narrowed.

"Where in New York?"

Paola gave him the address Aleida had given her. She had memorized it.

She held her breath. The agent continued to look at her. She could feel a bead of sweat trickle down her back.

Without a word, he handed her the passport and gave her a nod to let her go on her way.

She began to breathe again, collected her bag, and headed out into the arrivals area.

Tall, very white, and with curly red hair. That was how Aleida had described Thomas.

Paola scanned the crowds looking for someone who matched that description. She clutched her purse that held the toy frog and pulled the suitcase that contained all she now owned in the world.

She was exhausted and headed to a seat to wait. What if Thomas didn't come? She shook that thought from her head. He *had* to come. She didn't know another single person in the whole of North America.

Then she saw a head of red curly hair towering above the crowds. That must be Thomas. But Paola was suddenly afraid. Could she trust him? Could she trust anyone after what had happened to her?

Paola sat, hiding the frog. She wasn't ready. She wasn't ready to leave her old life behind. She had so many dreams for her future in Colombia, and now, in a matter of days, all that had changed. Here she was, sitting in a strange airport, watching a strange man who was going to take her to a strange apartment in a strange city.

After quite a while of sitting and watching, Paola realized that she would have to speak up eventually or else spend the night in the airport. And if Thomas left, then she would have nowhere to go. She pulled out the frog and set him on her lap. She saw Thomas catch sight of the toy and come over.

They introduced themselves clumsily as Thomas didn't speak Spanish and Paola only spoke a few words of English. Then Thomas motioned for her to follow him as he led the way to the subway trains to make their way into the city.

By the time they got to Thomas's apartment, Paola's senses were overloaded: the lights blazing from signs, windows, and headlights of taxis; the smells from restaurants and sewers; and the noise of car horns, engines, and people— people everywhere. It was a relief to get off the street.

When Thomas opened the door, Paola peered inside. It was tiny, much smaller than her own apartment back in Quimbaya. This one only had two rooms, not much furniture, and a funny smell.

Paola couldn't place the odour, it just smelled old and sad.

The first few days were unreal for Paola. Part of her was still back in Colombia. The rest of her was trying to come to terms with living in this foreign place. She barely left the apartment the first few days. The farthest she could bring herself to go was to the corner store. She desperately wanted to climb on a plane and head back home.

But she knew that was impossible. She did the next best thing.

"Hello?"

"Hello, Mamita?" Paola gripped the pay phone tightly and closed her eyes pretending she could see her grandmother standing in front of her.

"Paito! How are you? Where are you?" Her grandmother's voice sounded small and distant.

"I'm in New York." Even saying the words seemed unreal to Paola.

"Are you okay?" her grandmother asked.

Paola swallowed before answering. "I'm fine. Really."

"But how are you managing?" Her grandmother sounded close to tears.

"Don't worry, Mamita. I have a place to stay with Aleida's friend, Thomas. I'm going to start looking for a job and I'll have my own place before you know it," Paola said with a confidence she didn't really feel.

They talked for a few more minutes and then she said goodbye to her grandmother. The call was expensive and she only had $300 to live on for the time being. And truthfully, she didn't know where to begin looking for a job.

The pay phone was outside of the corner store and Paola decided to grab some chips before heading back to the apartment.

A poster taped to the window caught her eye. It was written in Spanish. It was an ad for a talk on empowerment, which was something Paola was definitely interested in. It was the whole idea behind what she had been trying to do as Family Commissioner in Quimbaya—empowering people to take control of their lives, find refuge from abuse, and start over.

It would be interesting to hear what New Yorkers were saying. And even more exciting was that it was being held at the Colombian Civic Center. Paola didn't even know there was a Colombian Center, but it was encouraging to think that she might be able to meet other people who shared her language and culture. Maybe New York wouldn't feel so strange.

The event wasn't what Paola expected. This talk on empowerment dealt with getting energy from the universe. She felt anger and frustration rise inside her. With all the terrible things going on in the world, why weren't these people here to learn about empowering themselves with inner strength? Why weren't they talking about how to stop abuse and violence?

She couldn't hold it in any longer. She felt herself standing and giving her views on empowerment from a community service perspective. There was a murmur after she was done and when she sat down again, she was still trembling with emotion.

"Excuse me," a man said, sitting down next to her when the meeting was over, "but that was really inspiring."

Paola smiled.

"How long have you been here?"

"Only a few weeks," she said.

"Where are you working?"

"Well, actually I'm still looking for a job."

"I own a restaurant. If you like, you can work for me."

It was an offer she couldn't refuse. She started right away, grateful to be bringing in some money. But despite the fact that she was starting to get her feet under her, she knew that she needed to get some sort of official status with the government, or she would be considered an illegal immigrant soon. There was no way she wanted to live that life, taking only low-paying jobs because she didn't have the proper paperwork. Always looking behind her for immigration officials waiting to deport her.

It was an issue she brought up the next time she went to the Colombian Civic Center. She was told that a group of Colombians had already started the paperwork to petition the US government for Temporary Protected Status. That meant the government would allow Colombians who were already in the United States the right to remain because it was too dangerous for them to return.

Several countries, such as Nicaragua and Haiti, had already gained Protected Status because of wars or environmental disasters. People from those countries could not be deported and were eligible to find work and apply for permanent residency.

But Colombia wasn't on the list. So Paola joined the task force to help with the application to plead their case to the US government about the life-threatening violence, the corruption, and the terrifying danger for anyone forced to go back. Then it was just a waiting game. It could take months for the decision to come through, and in the meantime, Paola needed to make some money and find her own place to stay.

Working in a restaurant was a new experience for Paola. Not only did she have to pick up some working English quickly, but she was on her feet for hours. She was also used to being in a position of responsibility where she had respect and power. As a waitress she was sometimes treated like she was invisible, or worse, like a servant.

It was a pleasant surprise to meet not only a kind customer, but also one who spoke Spanish so she didn't have to struggle with her broken English.

"Hi," he said one day, giving her a smile. "You're new here."

"Yes, can I get you some coffee?"

"Sure. Thanks..." he peered at her name tag, "...Paola. I'm Jesus." He pronounced it the Spanish way as "Hey-Zeus."

It was easy to strike up a conversation with him and Paola found herself looking forward to seeing him come in to the restaurant. When he asked her out on a date, she said yes. Paola hadn't realized how lonely she was without her friends and family, and Jesus was very kind to her. She enjoyed his company and they spent more and more time together.

But then, her world came crashing down again.

"What's wrong?" Jesus asked her one night, noticing how unusually quiet and withdrawn she was.

"Everything."

"Everything? What do you mean? It can't be that bad," he said.

Paola took a deep breath.

"I'm pregnant."

Chapter 10

Paola moved through the weeks in a daze. She kept working at the restaurant and tried to block out the complications of her life and just focus on living minute by minute.

A couple of months later she had saved enough money to rent her own place in an area of New York City called Astoria in Queens. It was an apartment in a house, which suited her better than sharing space in Thomas' tiny apartment. She repainted the walls and tried to make it feel more home-like.

Paola had to face some hard truths—she was soon going to have another child to care for, and she had recently broken up with Jesus. The two remained good friends, but Paola had to figure out what she was going to do next all by herself. Should she risk her life and try and go back home to Colombia and raise her new child with the son she had had to leave behind?

Just thinking of Santiago made Paola break down. She missed him so much and felt so guilty about the way she'd had to leave him. She had told him she would see him the next morning, and she had just disappeared from his life. It broke her heart.

Then came another blow. When she arrived at the Colombian Civic Center for her volunteer duties, she heard the news. They had waited for months for the application for Colombia to be included in the Temporary Protected Status to be reviewed, but after all their hard work, it was denied. She had no status to stay in the United States. At some point, she would either have to live as an illegal immigrant or she would have to leave.

She called her mother to tell her the news.

"So, that's it," Paola said. "I've had it. I'm leaving."

"Leaving?" her mother said.

"Yes. My whole life is a mess. Our application for protected status was turned down, so I can't stay here. I left one child in Colombia, now I've got this child coming in a couple of months. I can't do this anymore. I'm coming home."

"Paola, you can't. It's too dangerous. You will be putting not only yourself at risk but also Santiago, us, and this new baby. You have to figure this out where you are."

It was hard to hear, but her mother was

right. This mess wasn't going to be cleaned up by running away. The decisions she had to make now were huge, life altering, and overwhelming. She decided that she had to take action. She *could* figure this out.

Paola headed to a nearby internet café. She needed to get online. She sat there, her fingers poised over the keyboard. What was she going to search for?

Refugees.

That was what she typed into the search bar. She hit enter.

A page with all kinds of links appeared. One near the top caught her eye. It was the Jesuit Refugee Service in Quebec, Canada. Paola clicked on the link. Up popped information on how the Jesuit priests strove to "accompany, serve and advocate for the rights of refugees and other forcibly displaced persons."

Sounds like me, Paola thought.

She called the number on the website.

"Hello?" a man's voice answered. "Father Jack Costello speaking."

"Yes, hello, I need to go to Canada."

There was silence on the other end of the phone.

"You need to come to Canada?" Father

Costello said, switching to Spanish when he heard Paola's accent.

"Yes, I need to get out of here."

"Where's 'here'?"

"I'm in New York."

"I'm sorry, but I can't send you any money."

"I'm not asking for money," Paola said, "I need information."

"Okay. I'm going to give you the number for Romero House."

"What is that?"

"It is a refugee shelter in Toronto. They help people who want to claim refugee status in Canada, and there is someone who speaks Spanish there."

Paola took down the number and made the call.

The woman on the other end was named Diana. After a brief conversation where Paola explained her situation, Diana told Paola to first look up Canada's *Immigration and Refugee Protection Act* online to see if she qualified. Then she could call her back and they would make arrangements.

Paola studied the *Immigration and Refugee Protection Act* line by line. She learned from Diana that in order to avoid deportation, she had to make an appointment with an immigration officer and claim protection.

"How do I do that?" she asked Diana in another phone call.

"There is an organization in Buffalo called Vive La Casa. It is the only organization that is allowed to set up those appointments."

"Where is Buffalo?"

"On the border with Fort Erie, Ontario."

Every name was strange and every city was farther away from Colombia, but Paola was determined to get her life in order and feel safe. Maybe Canada would be that place.

Paola called Vive La Casa and asked to set up the appointment.

"You can't set up an appointment unless you are here, in person," the woman on the phone told her.

"But I live in New York," Paola said.

"You have to come and stay here while you wait," the woman said.

"But I am pregnant and almost due. I need to be near my doctor and the hospital."

"Oh, you can't come until after you have the baby then. Once you start this process, you have to be available to leave right away."

Paola thanked her and hung up. Trying not

to sound as disappointed as she felt, she called Diana at Romero House again and told her she had to wait until the baby was born to come.

"We'll be here," Diana told her. "Let me know when you get to Buffalo."

"I will."

It was going to be hard to wait but maybe it would give her time to get used to the idea of what was to come: Travel to Buffalo. Cross into Fort Erie. Make her way to Toronto.

Will I ever stop moving? she wondered.

The first time Paola laid eyes on her newborn son, Matthew, she thought he was perfect and her heart filled with love. He deserves a life free from fear and violence, she thought. And if that meant jumping through hoops to emigrate, then that's what she was going to do.

Matthew was only a few months old when she packed up her apartment and bought a plane ticket to Buffalo. After a short flight she took a taxi to Vive La Casa, but it was so early, even the staff hadn't arrived.

When she was finally let in, the woman checked all Paola's paperwork to see if it was in order. Then she explained how things at Vive La Casa worked.

"Here is the chore book," the woman said briskly. "You pick the chore you want to do and when you're done, you get a meal ticket."

Paola chafed at the idea of having to do chores in order to eat.

"What about restaurants nearby?" Paola asked. She had a suitcase full of formula and diapers for Matthew, so he was okay, but she was hungry and had a bit of money.

"There is nothing around here."

"There has to be something."

"No, it's too dangerous a neighbourhood for you to be walking around, especially with a baby."

Paola didn't know what to say, because she didn't know her way around and didn't want to put Matthew in danger.

"How can I do chores? I have a baby," Paola said to the woman.

"Then find someone to look after him. No chores, no food." The woman turned her back. It was obvious the conversation was over.

Paola took her suitcase and went to her room. She passed people in the hallway but hugged Matthew close. They were of all different nationalities and total strangers to her. There was no way in the world she was leaving Matthew with someone she didn't know.

That left her with the problem of not eating. She noticed another woman who was arguing with the nun in charge and seemed unhappy with the arrangements at Vive La Casa.

Paola mentioned to the woman that she was thinking of going to a nearby hotel and waiting there and did she want to come along? The woman said yes and they made their way there.

When they arrived, Paola was astounded to see that most of the people staying there were Colombians and Venezuelans also looking to emigrate. It was like one big family. She could speak the same language and get to know them. And they adored Matthew. The only problem was she had to phone over to Vive La Casa every day to find out if she had an appointment. Day after day she called and every day was the same response...not yet.

Paola soon discovered that many of the people in the hotel trying to get into Canada didn't know the *Immigration and Refugee Protection Act* like she did. Her legal background meant she spent a lot of her time explaining things to others and helping them get everything in order.

It all seemed to be moving along until they got the news.

"What does it mean when they say they're going to 'close the border'?" one man asked Paola.

"Close the border? Where did you hear that?"

"From my friend. He said it had to do with the Safe Third Country Agreement."

Paola went to investigate. He was right. The governments of Canada and the US had signed an agreement that was going to come into effect soon. It stated that a claimant had to seek protection in the first safe country he or she arrived in. For Paola that would mean she would have to ask for asylum in the United States.

But the US government had already turned Colombia down for Protected Status so it was unlikely that they would approve her request after that. There was a good chance that if the border closed, she would not be allowed to stay in the US and would be sent back to Colombia.

It was a terrifying thought. They'd be sending her back to her certain death. The agreement was set to come into effect in a few months. Would she make it across in time? The wait for her appointment grew more intense.

Six weeks later, she got the news she had been waiting for. She had an appointment with the Canadian Immigration Service in Fort Erie on June 5th, 2004.

A taxi took her and Matthew on the ten-minute drive across the border into Canada. She was fingerprinted and then she had to wait for her interview. There was nothing to eat or drink except for pop and chips from the vending machinges. But despite the fact that she was very hungry, she wasn't sure she could use American coins in Canadian machines. And so she went without.

"Paola Gomez," an immigration officer called out to the waiting room.

Paola and Matthew made their way into a little room.

"So tell me why you are seeking protection in Canada?" the officer asked.

Paola's mind flashed through all the things that had happened: her job as Family Commissioner, the shelter, Wilfred, her denouncing the "cleansings" on the radio, the death threats, the brutal assault, and the promise that if they found her again, they would murder her. She began her tale.

"I was the Family Commissioner in a small town called Quimbaya in Colombia..."

Chapter 11

The clock read 3:30 in the afternoon. It had been an excruciatingly long day of interviews and waiting. Paola's shoulders ached from holding Matthew and sitting in the uncomfortable chairs, waiting for word on the immigration department's decision.

"Ms. Gomez?" a man called out.

Paola followed him into a little room, similar to the one where she answered all the questions about her life in Colombia and why she was claiming refugee status.

"You have been approved to start the process, and can proceed to..." he checked her file, "...Romero House."

"Thank you," Paola said, getting to her feet, a smile spreading across her face.

"Welcome to Canada," he said.

This is the happiest day, she thought as the van pulled away from the curb in Fort Erie for the hour-and-a-half drive to Romero House in Toronto. Matthew slept on her lap. It had been a long day for him, too, cooped up in the immigration centre.

It was already dark out when the van pulled onto Keele Street in Toronto and stopped in front of one of the homes that was run by Romero House. A young intern named Yenica met her and Matthew as they got out of the van.

"Welcome home," Yenica said.

Paola fought back tears.

Yenica took her upstairs to her new room. She would share the kitchen and bathroom with the other residents in the house, but one room was just for her. Pale blue walls and white linens made the room feel fresh and bright. There was even a crib for Matthew. Paola was overwhelmed.

"It's the prettiest place I have ever lived," she said in her broken English.

Yenica wished her a good night's rest in her new home.

"What about a key for my door?" Paola asked.

Yenica smiled. "We don't lock our doors here. We're family and you're home."

Home.

She hadn't used that word in a long time. But she *was* home. After more than a year of feeling displaced and out of control, she finally felt that she was able to make decisions about her life again. She had found safety, for her and her son.

There was a sack of potatoes on the dresser

that Yenica had mentioned was for her to eat, but Paola was too shy to venture into the kitchen where the other mothers might be cooking. She was hungry but she was even more tired. She put Matthew in the crib and she lay on her bed. In a moment she was asleep.

The next morning it took her a few minutes to realize where she was. Matthew was up and gurgling.

"Let's explore," Paola said to Matthew as she dressed him. She didn't have a stroller so she carried him in her arms. Near her house she came upon a yard with tables set up and all kinds of items laid out. People milled about, picking things up and putting them down again. A man wearing a short canvas tool apron was walking around talking to people.

Paola looked at all the items. Then her eye fell on a cute china cup on one of the tables.

"How much?" she asked the man who had come up to her.

"One dollar."

"Okay." Paola rooted around in her purse for the Canadian money she had exchanged in Fort Erie, all while trying to juggle Matthew in her other arm. Finally she pulled out a five-dollar bill.

The man took the cup and began wrapping

it in newspaper. He looked at the bill she was holding out to him.

"Do you have a loonie?" he asked.

Paola paused. Loonie? What was he asking? The only loonies she knew were the *Looney Tunes* shows she had seen on TV.

"I don't watch cartoons," she said.

The man looked startled for a moment before giving her four dollars in change.

Paola found small grocery stores nearby and bought a few things to make dinner. She didn't cook very well, but she didn't have enough money to be eating in restaurants all the time. She was going to have to learn.

Back at the house she bumped into Yenica.

"How are you settling in?" she asked Paola.

"Good. I think."

Yenica smiled. "It can be hard in a new place, but if there is anything you need, or if you just want to talk, I'm here."

"Um, I have a question. I was shopping at a sale at someone's house..."

"A garage sale?"

"It wasn't in a garage."

"Well, sometimes it's called a yard sale. Did you find something?"

Paola pulled out the pretty little china cup.

"That's lovely," Yenica said.

"Yes, but why did the man ask me if I like cartoons?"

"Cartoons? What did he say exactly?"

"He asked if I like Looney. Or if I have Looney. Something like that."

Yenica smiled. "That's not a cartoon, that's money. The one dollar coin is called a loonie."

"Oh." Paola felt heat rising to her cheeks. "Maybe the first thing I do is learn English better."

"Well, there is a good program at the Bickford Centre. I can get you the information if you like."

Paola nodded. She had only picked up broken English during her time in New York. If she was going to make a go of it here, she was going to have to be able to communicate more effectively.

There was another reason Paola needed to improve her English. She was going to contact immigration officials to find out how to go about helping Matthew's father, Jesus, come to Toronto. She did not want Matthew to grow up without the love and support of both his parents. And it was important for her to be clear with government officials about their situation.

A few weeks later Paola went to the Bickford Centre to register for English classes. She walked up to the registration desk.

"I want to enter the English lesson?" Paola said.

"What do you want?" the secretary asked, looking annoyed.

Paola tried to explain again that she wanted to register for English classes.

The secretary asked her to repeat herself several times, her tone of voice getting sharper and ruder.

Finally the woman said, "I don't understand you. I am sick and tired of people not speaking proper English!"

Paola turned away from the counter and walked out of the office. She sat down on the floor in the corridor and started crying. It all seemed too difficult—she was trying so hard to fit in, to find her way, to build a new life and in one moment, all the courage and strength she had gathered had drained out of her. She felt defeated.

"Are you all right?" A woman had come over to Paola and bent down to speak to her. She told Paola she was a teacher at the school and asked her what happened.

Through her tears Paola managed to tell her how hard she had tried to register and how rude the secretary had been. The woman put a hand on her shoulder. "Please don't take it personally. Some people have many reasons to be happy but they choose to be miserable. The person who treated you badly doesn't deserve your tears. You are coming to English classes because you need to learn. In fact, it is because of you that she even has a job!"

The woman laughed at this and Paola ended up laughing, too. The teacher took her to a different secretary who helped Paola get registered.

English classes were going well, if a bit slow. Paola found herself impatient with the pace of classes. She knew she could learn so much faster, but there were others in the class who were struggling and the lessons had to move at their speed.

Good news came about a month later—Jesus was given permission to join them in Toronto. It was a happy reunion and Jesus couldn't believe how much Matthew had grown in the few months since he had seen him last. Now that there were three of them, the people at Romero House moved Paola, Jesus, and Matthew into a bachelor apartment. Jesus was also eager to improve his

English and began taking language classes. He was hoping to get into the construction trade.

English classes touched on many topics of interest to new immigrants and refugees. In one class the topic turned to Canada's laws and how they might be different from other countries. The talk turned to same-sex marriage and the teacher explained that it was legal in Canada.

A male student stood up and said, "If I had a gay child, I would put him in jail!"

Paola was shocked. She couldn't understand how such opinions were still held by people. And how could he say that? she wondered. Didn't he come to Canada precisely *because* it was an open and free country where everyone was supposed to be treated equally and protected equally under the law?

Paola waited for the teacher to say something, but she didn't. Paola stood up.

"Teacher, he needs to take his statement back and I feel really afraid for what he is saying."

Still the teacher said nothing.

The man answered Paola angrily, "If you are lesbian, you are not my problem, but my sons are my problem so yes, I put him in jail!"

Paola was trembling. She demanded the teacher do something, but nothing happened.

Paola gathered her books and left. She didn't want to be in the room with such ignorance, and worse still, she was appalled that the teacher said and did nothing to stop it.

Paola went back to Romero House, crying. An intern met her at the door and took her to a quiet room where they could talk. She told him what had happened at school.

"It is unacceptable that this man is trying to bring his backward ideas into this country, but he will have to live by our laws whether he wants to or not. But why has it upset you so much that you are trembling?" he asked her.

"It reminds me of how things were in Colombia," Paola said. "People were not protected just because they were different. I had an uncle..." she swallowed hard. "...who was severely beaten because of his sexual orientation."

Paola dried her eyes. "I am never going back to that school," she said.

The realization hit her, that even here in her adopted country there was work to be done. Prejudice and injustice were everywhere in the world and even though she was safe now, maybe there was still ways she could help. It was time to get involved again.

Chapter 12

"Hi, Diana," Paola said. "It's Paola Gomez. Do you remember me?"

It had been a while since they'd spoken. Diana had left her job at Romero House and found another position.

"Of course! How are you doing? I'm sorry I'm not at Romero House anymore. How are you settling in?"

"Good. Jesus is with me now and I've been taking English lessons."

"Excellent. Well, how can I help?"

"I was wondering...I know you are working for the FCJ Refugee Centre and I was wondering if there was any volunteer work there?"

"You know," Diana said after a pause, "someone with your legal background might be helpful. Let me see what I can do."

Paola knew that the FCJ Refugee Centre worked with women and child refugee claimants as well as other uprooted people. She was very excited when Diana called her back and said that they could certainly use her expertise as a volunteer.

Paola was put to work helping new refugee claimants navigate the murky waters of Immigration and Refugee Law. With her law degree from Colombia and all the reading she had done while she was waiting for her own immigration interview in Buffalo (she read the entire *Immigration and Refugee Protection Act*), she could unravel the little legal details and properly prepare people to state their cases for admittance.

Her English was still a little rough but an interpreter at the centre named Carlos helped her out by taking the documents she had written and editing them in a red pen. By fixing her mistakes with Carlos, her English improved by leaps and bounds.

A few months after she first started, Diana left the FCJ and Paola was offered the position of office coordinator. She accepted gratefully. It felt good to be working in a job of responsibility again as she dealt with the legal aspects and support of clients.

For two years, Paola continued in her job and felt she was doing good work, but she wanted to do more. She knew that women refugees faced special difficulties in immigrating. She recognized that not everyone had the strong skills and strong will that she did. She also realized that Latin American women had cultural and language differences that might make them more vulnerable to manipulation or abuse. Like many of the women she helped back in Quimbaya, they might not know their legal rights.

When Paola heard of a job opening up at the YWCA helping abused women, she dropped off a resume. A few days later she got called for an interview with the manager.

"So, you're interested in the position we advertised for someone with a background in immigration who will be working with women experiencing violence. Is that correct?" the woman asked, scanning Paola's resume.

Paola nodded.

The woman looked up. "And do you have that background?"

"I am an immigrant myself, so I know what a huge deal it is to leave your home and how frightening it can be."

The woman leaned back in her chair. "Lots of people are immigrants. It doesn't necessarily make you a candidate to help them."

"I'm also a lawyer."

"You are? You have credentials?" The woman asked, scanning her resume.

"I qualified in Colombia. They haven't accepted my designation here."

"Oh, well that's still impressive. But these women are the victims of abuse. How are you qualified to help them?"

"I was the Family Commissioner in my town in Colombia. I worked with many, many victims of abuse and violence. I also opened and ran a shelter for street kids."

The woman smiled. "When can you start?"

Paola dove into her work. It felt good to be making a difference again. And the women's stories were all too familiar. Now, at least, Paola could offer them the hope that they would be safer and have more legal protection here than in their home countries. It was almost as if she had come full circle. And as she worked with families around the city, it reminded her of her own scattered family and the child always on her mind and in her heart, but missing from her life—Santiago.

That hole was filled the day she waited in Fort Erie and watched as her mother and Santiago crossed the border into Canada. Would he recognize her?

"Santi!" she called when he came into view.

He looked at her for a moment, as if searching

her face for something familiar. Then he broke into a wide smile and ran into her arms. He was there to stay. For the first time in years Paola felt complete, like all the little pieces of her life were finally put back into place.

Chapter 13

All the time she was helping the women in her new job, Paola also saw the children—youngsters torn from their homes and living in the unfamiliar and crowded shelters. Fear was the one constant in their lives: fear of the violence that had plagued their families, fear of leaving, fear of having nothing, and fear of starting over. She saw the same in the refugee children coming through Romero House.

She had to do something. She knew most of the programs at shelters were aimed at helping the women who were escaping horrible situations. *But what about the kids they brought with them?* Paola asked herself. She knew how much the children suffered when their parents were going through turmoil. Memories of the New Dawn shelter flooded her mind.

The thing that had made the shelter kids' lives bearable were the many programs she and her staff had implemented. Their favourite activities were the art projects they would work on. The children felt free to express themselves through art and it often led to conversations, revelations, and inspiration.

Paola knew this from personal experience, too. Now that she felt a little more settled, she had gone back to writing poetry. Her poems spoke of love, heartbreak, struggles, and despair. They offered her experiences as a woman, mother, friend, and social activist. She called her collection, *El Alma Mia,* which means "My Soul," and she wanted something striking for the cover art.

"Hello? Is this Alex Usquiano?" Paola asked, hoping her long-distance call to Colombia wouldn't be too expensive.

"Yes."

"You don't know me, but my name is Paola Gomez and I was wondering if I could hire you to do a small piece of artwork for me? I think you are really talented."

"Well, thank you, but I *do* know you."

"You do?"

"Sure, I came to work for you at the New Dawn Shelter. I helped with the kids' art program."

Paola wracked her brain to remember. "Oh, is that so?"

Alex laughed. "You don't remember me, do you?"

"Well, we had a lot of artists coming and going…"

"I was mostly going. You fired me."

Paola was glad that they were speaking on the phone and not in person so Alex couldn't see how red her face was.

"I'm sorry…"

Alex laughed again. "No problem. Now, what did you have in mind for this artwork?"

Paola described her book to him and Alex agreed to create the cover for her book of poetry. They kept in touch over the following weeks while Alex worked and their conversations came around to Paola's belief in the importance of art for the most vulnerable people in society.

"Even here," she said, "I see kids in situations of distress and transition, both refugees and shelter kids. They remind me of the kids at the New Dawn Shelter."

"Then we should create a program like you had here in Colombia," Alex told her.

"You mean an art program for shelter kids?"

"Exactly."

"You know, it could be wonderful for them. Let's make it happen."

Together they came up with the program details such as which media they would use and how they would present them.

Paola searched for a name for the art program. She knew that a "muse" was an ancient Greek term for a goddess who was a source of inspiration for the creative arts. She thought that would fit well. But her own inspiration was missing and she had not been able to be creative because of her own experiences—her muse was sick, she thought. It needed to be pampered and cared for, like the children in the program did. Sick Muse was born.

Paola wanted an art program that would not only just let kids be creative but would also give them the opportunity to talk about diversity, inclusion, and social justice. And it could be a chance for kids to just be kids for a while.

When Paola got something in her mind, she ran with it. With Alex still in Colombia, she used her own money to head to the store to buy art supplies: markers, paper, pens, and pencils.

She held the first Sick Muse art session at a transitional housing complex. These homes provided temporary living quarters for families before they moved to permanent, safe homes. There were twenty kids at that first session and Paola came away from the experience knowing this was going to be something special. She hoped her funds would hold out so she could bring the program to more children.

As she and Alex continued to phone back and forth, Paola knew they had a special connection. She was able to sponsor Alex to come to Canada where their relationship deepened into love, and they married.

As well as co-founding Sick Muse, Alex continued to create his artwork and wanted to put on an exhibit called *The Art of Non-Violence.* It was expensive to put on a show, but Paola heard that there might be funding available.

Paola called the Toronto Arts Council. She described the art exhibit but was disappointed to hear that the deadline for applying for a grant had already passed. But as she talked with the staff member, Andrew, the conversation turned to the Sick Muse program at the shelters and Romero House.

"We explore painting, sculpture, photography, and paper maché. We don't talk about healing, we just hang out. But we direct the conversation to diversity and inclusion."

"Give me an example."

"Well, we might talk about building community together, such as 'Today, let's think about nature and the beautiful landscape in the city that you like.' So each child works on part of the landscape; they are part of a whole."

"That is a fantastic idea," Andrew said. "I know lots of kids who are in a difficult situation who would love this program. Why aren't you taking it to more places?"

"Because I cannot afford to at this time," Paola replied. "All the supplies come out of my pocket."

"You know, there is another grant for projects like this and that deadline hasn't passed. Why don't you apply for funding for your arts program?"

Paola was thrilled. Instead of relying on the bit of money she could spare, the program could expand to include photography and sculpture. Our World of a Thousand Colours was one of the programs she developed once she had funding. It celebrates art while talking about diversity and the beauty that comes with it.

Paola and a dedicated staff of volunteers now had the resources to reach many more kids. They took their program to shelters, transitional housing centres, and community centres. The children were all in a time of confusion and change in their lives, whether foster kids, shelter kids, or refugees. For a little while each week, they could forget their situations and focus on learning a new skill, celebrating their creativity, and sharing who they were with others.

At the end of the program each day they would sit in a circle with the kids and share their day. Most kids expressed how they enjoyed learning a new skill but sometimes hurtful things would come out during circle time.

"I am very sad because I won't be here for Christmas. I am going to be deported," one boy told the group.

Paola felt her heart tighten. It hurt her to think that so much pain and fear had to be endured by someone so little. So she and the other staff members decided that they would celebrate Christmas early so he could participate. It filled her heart to see the joy on his face and reminded her of the importance of giving these kids all the attention she could because there was no guarantee that they would be there the next day.

This reinforced within Paola the need for families to be together and also the problems facing refugees like herself. She had worked to convince the Toronto Arts Council that refugee kids needed more attention. She began the process of creating a program for artists to partner with them to work with refugee kids to explore music, drama, pottery, and other artistic media.

Today, Paola is also committed to helping women in crisis. She speaks at seminars and performs research around the region on how to help Latin American women who have experienced violence. Her workshops teach workers how to be culturally sensitive and to understand that Latin American women come from many different countries, each with its own history and culture. She was thrilled to be recognized when she received the Amina Malko Award from Canadian Centre for Victims of Torture (CCVT) as well as the Constance E. Hamilton Award for her work securing equitable treatment for women in Toronto.

Paola's love of poetry and writing led her to connect with PEN Canada and its Writers in Exile Program. Members would gather regularly at Romero House. This international program supports writers, journalists, poets and others who have been forced to leave countries where they did not have freedom of expression. Paola wanted to help others explore social justice with their writing, and so she hosted creative writing workshops as PEN Canada's Writer-in-Residence for 2014.

Paola is looking to the future and still finding ways to help others. The Sick Muse art program is a finalist for the 2016 TD Arts Diversity Awards and Paola herself has been nominated as one of the "10 Most Influential Hispanic-Canadians." She is also part of a team of ten people preparing to launch the Sick Muse online magazine. It will be a showcase for anyone who works with refugee kids or is an emerging artist who deals with inclusion in the Arts.

Paola believes that collective work is more effective than individual work. She shows that belief with her collaborative art projects and art programs. She thinks we all deserve to have space in this world and an opportunity to reach our full potential. Through her continued work she wants to show that we can build a community together and make the world a better place.

Timeline

March 4, 1977 — Paola is born in Quimbaya, Colombia

March 1989 — Grade 7 project on a shelter for women and children

September 1994 — Paola begins law program at Universidad Le Gran Colombia

March 1998 — Paola becomes Family Commissioner

April 1998 — First radio program of "Family Commissioner at Your Home"

January 25, 1999 — Earthquake near Armenia, Colombia

April 1999 — Paola meets baby Santiago

June 1999 — Opening of New Dawn Shelter in Quimbaya

July 2000 — Paola finishes her law degree

May 2001 — Death of shelter child Wilfred

November 19, 2001 — Paola is attacked on her way to Pereira

November 21, 2001 — Flight to New York City, US, from Colombia

December 2003 — Birth of son Matthew

April 2004 — Paola arrives in Buffalo, New York to wait for her immigration interview

June 5, 2004 — Paola and Matthew cross into Canada

July 2004 — Jesus joins Paola and Matthew in Toronto

September 2004 — Paola volunteers at the FCJ Refugee Centre

December 29, 2004 — Border between Canada and the US now under new regulations of Safe Third Country Agreement

February 2005	Paola becomes office coordinator at FCJ
December 2005	Santiago arrives in Canada
December 2005	Paola receives word that her refugee status has been approved
October 2007	Paola begins work at YWCA
July 2008	Paola receives Vital People grant from Toronto Community Foundation
November 2009	Paola receives Amina Malko Award from Canadian Centre for Victims of Torture
January 2012	Paola becomes PEN Canada Writer-in-Exile
April 2012	Paola reunites with old friend and colleague Alex Usquiano
September 2012	Paola publishes poetry book, *El Alma Mia*
October 2012	Paola co-founds Sick Muse Art Project with partner, Alex Usquiano
November 2014	Paola is named PEN Canada Writer-in-Residence at George Brown College
May 2016	Sick Muse is named one of three finalists for the TD Arts Diversity Awards
June 2016	Paola is nominated for the 10 Most Influential Hispanic-Canadians Award
July 2016	Paola wins the Constance E. Hamilton Award from the City of Toronto Access, Human Rights and Equity Awards

Resources

More about Paola

Sick Muse Art Project:
www.sickmuseartprojects.org

Sick Muse Online Art Magazine:
www.sickmusemag.com

CBC audio interview about Romero House with Paola Gomez and Prince Munemo:
www.cbc.ca/news/canada/toronto/programs/metromorning/romero-house-1.3554987

Romero House refugee shelter:
www.romerohouse.org

PEN Canada Writers-in-Exile Program:
www.pencanada.ca/programs/writers-in-exile/

More about Life in Colombia

Books:

Cameron, Sara. *Out of War: True Stories from the Frontlines of the Children's Movement for Peace in Colombia.* Scholastic, 2001.

Croy, Anita. *National Geographic Countries of the World: Colombia.* National Geographic Children's Books, 2008.

Websites:

Video footage of Armenia, Colombia after the earthquake in 1999:

www.vimeo.com/9428771

TIME for Kids explores Colombia:

http://www.timeforkids.com/destination/colombia

Children's Rights in Colombia:

www.humanium.org/en/americas/colombia/

How Kids Can Help

Covenant House runs shelters for homeless youth in Toronto, Vancouver, Detroit, New York City, and 18 other sites across North America and Central America. Events such as Sleep Out raise funds for the shelter. There are also volunteer opportunities:
www.covenanthousetoronto.ca/homeless-youth/Home.aspx

SPARK Ontario helps connect people with volunteer opportunities to help refugees settle in Ontario:
www.findmyspark.ca/warmwelcome

Toronto Friends of Refugees works to resettle UNHCR-identified refugees to Canada. Those wanting to help can purchase a t-shirt, attend fundraising events, or volunteer:
www.tofriendsofrefugees.ca

I

Acknowledgements

Thanks to:

Paola Gomez for sharing her powerful story, for being so prompt in answering my questions so I could meet my deadlines, and for never laughing at my horrible pronunciation of Spanish words.

Solange Messier and Christie Harkin for their belief in the importance of bringing these stories to young readers and for their faith in my ability to do so.

Alex, Chelsey, Nathan, and Haley for keeping me grounded and being my cheerleaders when I begin to doubt.

And especially Craig, who picked up the slack without complaint to keep everything running smoothly so I had the time to tackle this project.

- Natalie Hyde

Index

10 Most Influential Hispanic-Canadians, 131, 133

2016 TD Arts Diversity Awards, 131, 133

abusive home, 12–13, 14–18, 33–34

Aldana, Maria, 36, 47

Aleida, 89, 90, 91, 93

Alex Usquiano, 124–127, 133

Amina Malko Award, 130, 133

Ana Maria, 53–54, 63–68, 72

art, 18, 67, 74, 123–124, 125–131

attack on Paola, 85–88, 132

Bickford Centre, 113

Buffalo, NY, 103–104, 119, 132

Canadian Centre for Victims of Torture (CCVT), 130, 133

Christian, 37–38

City of Toronto Access, Human Rights and Equity Awards, 133

cleansings, 51, 61, 67–69, 70, 72–74, 75–76, 108,

Colombian Civic Center, 94–95, 100,

Constance E. Hamilton Award, 130, 133,

Costello, Father Jack, 101

Diana, 102–104, 118–119

earthquake, 38–49, 61, 132

Edgar, 34, 51–52, 55–57, 60–62

El Alma Mia, 124, 133

English-as-a-second-language classes, 113–117

Eugenia, 65

Family Commissioner in Your Home, 33–34, 52–53, 74–76, 82, 132

father, Paola's, 12, 13, 15–17, 19–20, 21–28, 70–71,

FCJ Refugee Centre, 118–119, 132, 133

fear, 42, 50, 80, 81, 86–89, 104, 123, 129,

Fernando, 37–39

flight to Buffalo, 104

flight to New York City, 90–91

Fort Erie, ON, 103, 104, 108, 121,

Immigration and Refugee Protection Act, 102, 106, 119

Immigration Canada, 10, 108, 109

immigration to Canada, 109–110

Jairo's Place Restaurant, 37

Jesuit Refugee Service, 101

Jesus, 97–98, 99, 113, 115, 118, 132

Juan, 53–55, 56, 68–69

Mamita, 14–17, 20, 27–30, 36–38, 40, 48, 93–94

Matthew, 104, 105, 106, 108–111, 115, 132

Mondragon, Cesar, 36, 47–48

Monica, 13–14

Moore, Thomas, 89, 90–92, 93, 99

mother, Paola's, 12, 14, 17, 20, 33, 34, 37, 39, 40,
        44, 65–66, 71, 80–82, 83, 84, 87–88, 100, 121

music, 18, 53–55, 130

murder, 50, 61, 72–73, 74, 76,

Naranjo, Carlos, 36, 47–48

New Dawn Child Protection Centre, 49–50, 62,
        123–124, 125, 132

New York City, 90–104

Operation Friendship, 58

Oscar, 37, 41

Osorio, James, 36, 48

Our World of a Thousand Colours, 128

PEN Canada, 130, 133

        Writers in Exile, 130, 133

poetry, 12, 27, 48, 70, 124–125, 130

Romero House, 102, 104, 109–111, 115, 117,
        118, 123, 127, 130

Safe Third Country Agreement, 107, 132

Santiago, 64–66, 70–71, 80, 81, 83, 85, 88,
        99–100, 121–122, 132

Sebastian, 39, 43

school project, 12–14, 17–18

Sick Muse Art Project, 126–127, 131, 133

social justice, 13–14, 30, 33–35, 51–53, 58, 76,
        116–117, 126, 130

Temporary Protected Status, 96, 100

threats, 52, 75, 76, 82, 86, 108

Toronto Arts Council, 127–128, 129

Toronto Community Foundation, 133

Toronto, Ontario, 108–131

Universidad Le Gran Colombia, 19, 22, 42

Vital People Grant, 133

Vive La Casa, 10, 103, 104–106

Wilfred, 57, 58–59, 62–63, 68–69, 70, 72–74,
        75–76, 108, 118–122, 128–131, 132

YWCA, 120, 133

Also available in the Arrivals series

STAY STRONG
A Musician's Journey
from Congo

Natalie Hyde